BELLE

SISTER WITCHES OF STORY COVE, BOOK 2

NYX HALLIWELL

CHAPTER

ONE

Books talk to me.

I don't mean metaphorically. They actually speak to me and tell me all sorts of things. Places they've been, people who've read them—or those who didn't, leaving them on a dark shelf or tossing them in the garbage. At times characters come alive to me, and sometimes the voice of the author does as well. I've heard all kinds of tales from them, and while most are comforting, involving the people who loved and respected them, others can be quite disturbing.

Which is why I rescue as many of those as I can.

I take them to Beanstalk Books where I'm employed part-time. We carry gently used volumes, as well as new works of fiction and non. A few end up at the town library, which is always understaffed and on a strict budget. I volunteer there once a month, and we can use all the donations we can get.

On this beautiful, late September morning, I stroll up the hill to the Kingsley Mansion on Millionaires Row, north of downtown. I've left my sister, Ruby, in charge of The Enchanted Candle & Soap Company, the family business my three siblings and I own, to meet with a man who may be able to help us expand.

At least I hope so. The old books I have to show him are heavy, and I'm optimistic they'll be worth something. They're dead silent, refusing to say a word even when I tickle them with my magick.

Walking beside me is my Pekingese, Jayne Eyre, who busily sniffs the sidewalk, bushes, and trees with her flat nose. The breeze ruffles her blond hair, a match for mine, and she wags her tail and barks hello at folks we pass out on their front porches or strolling by. Many stop to pet and make a fuss over her, which she eats up.

Working at Beanstalk is the perfect job, especially because it's next door to Enchanted. Jayne goes everywhere with me, including the library. Kids visit to read to her, and she's good with adults as well. Honestly, Jayne gets along with everyone. I try to do the same.

My appointment with Leo Kingsley has me excited and a tad nervous. He's a handsome millionaire I met at an informal dinner a few weeks ago who's rather eccentric but also exceptionally knowledgeable about vintage and antique items. He's sparked a well of creativity I didn't realize I had, bringing fresh ideas to a romance I'm penning, and he's set my terribly romantic heart beating to a new, if turbulent, rhythm.

He's the expert I need to appraise the volumes currently in my backpack. They're from a stash my sister, Cinder, uncovered when she began renovating our shop. In the turret of our house, we found a secret room containing our great-great-grandmother, Eunice's, office, complete with dozens of her personal journals and an extraordinary collection of odd books from the eighteen hundreds.

It was a secret fantasy come true for me, finding such rare and unusual books, and I've begun to hear what I can only believe is her voice whenever I'm near them. She founded Enchanted and there are stacks of her soap and candle recipes, along with the day-to-day accounts of the store. My sisters and I are slowly working our way through all of it.

While I wish to keep them all because parting with any is difficult, we are in need of funds for the remodeling, and the books I've culled from our grandmother's library don't seem to fit with the rest.

Eunice started the company in order to feed her family after her husband died, and my sisters and I continue to live and work there. We're hoping to expand what little space we have and carry a complete line of bath and body products soon, but remodeling takes cash.

Mr. Kingsley is known far and wide for his extensive library collection. Being an accomplished broker for vintage and antique books must aid his acquisitions. This morning, as I breath in the crisp September air, I'm excited to show him what I've brought, but in all honesty, I'm equally so to see him and get a peek at his reputed library.

Our brief conversation and interaction last month at famous actress Tiffany Starling's left me yearning to know more. He stays in his enormous mansion all the time, and I wonder why. He's handsome and wise, and although people find him a bit gruff and taciturn, I can't believe he enjoys staying cooped up inside that huge place.

While I'm an extrovert, I understand how a fantastic library might keep one at home. However, I feel there's a deeper story when it comes to him than simply being an eccentric millionaire. There's a mystery there, and there's nothing I love more—outside of books and my sisters—than a good secret.

I have one of my own. I wish with all my heart I could buy Beanstalk and combine it with Enchanted, opening the walls between the two Gothic houses to create a haven for people to curl up and relax with a good book, then take home an assortment of products to keep them happy.

My current hours are meager and the elderly owner, Daisy Marple, is in her seventies and having health issues. She relies on me to keep the place open and running on days she needs rest. Stress is beginning to get to her as the property is prime downtown space and developers want to buy her out, but she hates that idea as much as I do. We'd lose the only bookstore for miles.

I want to tell Cinder, Ruby, and Zelle about my

dream, but even with our recent increase in sales, thanks to Tiffany and her son, Finn, we don't have enough to purchase it.

Yet, being an optimist, I aspire to find a way.

Jayne and I pause to speak to Mrs. Derringer, the lady who lives near the park and heads our yearly fall festival in October. She's out for her morning jog and greets Jayne with an ear scruff. "Beautiful day, isn't it? I'm meeting your cousin this afternoon to order cider for next month. I estimate we'll need more than our usual hundred gallons."

That's great news for Snow and her apple orchard.

"I can't wait." I heft the backpack higher on my shoulder. "Fall is my favorite time of year, and I know Snow's excited, too. She's expecting more sightseers for Fairytale Land, and the giant pumpkin is up over five-hundred pounds! Between that and the downtown walk, it's going to be amazing. You do such a great job with it."

She jogs in place, a bright smile lighting her face, even as she waves off the compliment. "As you do running the book fair. I'm hoping to swing by this week and stock up on historical romances to read this winter."

"It's going to be our biggest ever."

"Is it true that Paul and Tonya Benning are doing a reading Saturday?"

The annual Wandering Words traveling book fair and author event draws crowds from all over the state. Story Cove is one of a dozen towns lucky enough to be on the month-long schedule, and it culminates with an author reading at Beanstalk Books. It's the biggest year ever for us—I hope. I can't tell anyone, but my magick may have had a bit to do with that coup.

It'll bring in buyers from all over Georgia and bolster the store's coffers, my secret plan to keep Daisy solvent. "They have a huge following locally since their books are set in a fictional town that mirrors ours, and I expect the store to be packed. Be sure you arrive early to get a good seat!"

She assures me she will, kisses Jayne's flat nose and resumes her pace once more.

As I draw closer to Millionaires Row, my nerves tingle and my chest feels tight with the thought of seeing Leo. It's not that he's ill mannered—quite the contrary—but he can be kind of...surly. I don't think he likes people much, and this again makes me wonder why. What is he hiding?

As Jayne and I climb the steep hill and stop outside the gated entrance to his mansion, I catch my breath, feeling my pulse skipping fast. My eyes take in the beauty of the turning maples and colorful bushes lining the wide yard. The double iron gates stand open, and we wend our way under the canopy of ancient oaks arching over the drive, sunlight dancing at our feet.

Jayne does more sniffing, making me pause here and there, the birds overhead seeming to greet us.

The landscape is lush. Three stories sprawl over the grounds in a plantation style layout with a wide veranda. Several concrete urns nearly as tall as I am stand guard at the bottom of the stairs. At the corners of the roof, bronze gargoyles watch us climb the steps to the front door.

There's no doorbell, only a brass knocker with the face of a lion. I can barely lift it, it's so heavy. It falls with a loud *thunk*.

I lift and let it fall a second time, Jayne sitting at my feet and looking up with expectation.

"Behave yourself," I tell her. "As soon as we're done here, we'll head to the bookstore."

She wags her tail, understanding in her eyes.

The door opens and a man dressed in a somber gray wool jacket and dark slacks greets us. "Ah, you're a few minutes early. I like punctuality."

I glance at my watch, noting we are exactly on time. "I appreciate Mr. Kingsley seeing us this morning."

His gaze drops to Jayne. "It would be better for the animal to wait outside. Perhaps no one has ever mentioned it to you, but professionalism dictates leaving your pet at home rather than allowing it to accompany you on a job interview."

"Job interview?"

His hair is graying at the temples, several lines etched in his forehead that seem cavernous as he frowns. "The curator position?"

I laugh. "I'm sorry, I'm not applying for any job. I'm Belle Sherwood. I made an appointment to see him about appraising some books."

The lines lift and he brightens. "Apologies. He didn't tell me you were coming." He gives me a slight bow. "I'm Albert, Mr. Kingsley's butler." He points at Jayne. "Regardless of the reason, Mr. Kingsley doesn't like dogs."

My stomach twists. Jayne goes everywhere with me, and this revelation is unwelcome. "How unfortunate."

"I'm afraid it would be best for him to wait outside."

I glance at my familiar and best friend. She cocks her head as if questioning Mr. Kingsley's good sense and I'm at war with myself over what to do. I don't want to offend the man, but I'm not leaving my dog on his porch.

"It's *her*. Jayne." I pull myself up to full size. "She's no ordinary dog, and she comes with me. She won't be any trouble, I promise."

Frowning once more, he looks us over, his high-brow air infecting the space. For a moment, I fear he's going to deny us entry.

Finally, he extends a hand, ushering us into the foyer.

Sunlight cascades from a second story arched window, illuminating black and white squares of marble. The entrance hall is as spacious as Enchanted's showroom, with forest green wallpaper on the top half of the walls and a burgundy version under a chair rail molding. Double staircases rise on either side to the second floor, creating a ceiling over the checkerboard floor squares that lead, I assume, to the rooms at the rear of the first level.

Albert directs me to the left and an enormous sitting room. "I'll advise Mr. Kingsley that you're here."

He exits and Jayne and I scan the well-appointed room. Wood paneling and green wallpaper that matches the hall give it a heavy, masculine appearance. The brick fireplace boasts a stained wood mantle with twin silver candlesticks. A gold framed portrait hangs above it featuring a couple in formal clothing.

While Jayne sniffs various pieces of antique furniture, I make my way toward the floor-to-ceiling shelves lining the far walls. Opening my psychic hearing, I'm disappointed when the books seem muffled. I can't understand them. Disappointed, I meander back to the fireplace.

As I study the portrait hanging there, I wonder if these are Leo's parents. I see some resemblance. They appear young in the picture, so full of life. Especially the woman, whose eyes seem extremely realistic, as if she's actually looking down at me.

I feel the tug of magick in the center of my chest and hear Jayne whine. Glancing over, I notice what seems to be a giant rose under a glass dome.

It turns its face toward me, and I wonder what kind of magick that is. My sister, Ruby, who has a penchant for herbs and flowers, would be delighted.

I move toward it, and the rose follows me as though it sees or senses my presence. Jayne whines again, and out of the corner of my eye, I swear I see the candlesticks on the mantle shift. When I twist to stare at them directly, they are once again inanimate.

A clock on a table near the sofa makes a noise. I face it and think I hear it chanting under its breath. An incantation?

Shifting closer, I feel my breathing become labored but the clock falls silent, not even ticking, as I peer at it.

In my peripheral vision, the candlesticks move.

Turning quickly in a circle, Jayne whining again, everything is as it should be, but as soon as I look away, the objects on the edge of my vision shift. When I return my attention to the rose, it seems to be wilting, and as soon as I step toward it, it comes to life again, the shade growing a vibrant ruby red.

A book on the end table near the clock catches my eye. From the cover I can tell it's as old as those in my backpack. I sense my grandmother's books inside shifting as I draw close to it. The title is faded gold and I have to lean in to see it, the clock making a soft sigh as I do.

"*Beasts and the Magick That Binds Them,*" I read aloud, tracing my fingers over the faded gold letters. I'm about to open the cover and see if it's anything like those in my backpack when it suddenly scoots away, slamming into the clock.

"Ouch!"

I jump back, Jayne becoming alert at my feet. A soft

growl issues from her throat. "Did you just...speak?" I ask the clock.

It sounds as if it mumbles something in reply, and before I can engage, or reach for the book, Albert appears. Jayne, still on alert, spins to face him as he enters the room, another growl on her lips.

He barely glances at her and gives me a restrained smile. "He'll see you now."

I'm almost grateful to leave the room, dragging in a fortifying breath as we walk down the long hall and stop at an elevator under the joint staircases. I hadn't realized I was holding my breath—or perhaps, I think, as air fills my lungs, the magick in there was sucking it out of me.

Albert hits a button, gives Jayne one more concerned look, then ushers us inside.

The doors close and Jayne and I are whisked up several floors. When they open and we step onto the third floor, once more my breath is taken away.

The famed Kingsley library is laid out in front of us in all of its beautiful grandeur.

CHAPTER

TWO

Alternating windows and bookshelves fill the space.

Sunlight streams through the arches in between the elegant, floor-to-ceiling shelves. Everywhere my gaze lands, I see books.

To my left is a giant desk containing stacks of volumes, a telephone, and a laptop. To my right is another fireplace, this one more modern, with a sitting area in front of it. On the coffee table and side tables are other books.

I'm literally speechless for several long moments, the distant sound of a man's voice barely registering as my hearing picks up the thousands of stories speaking at once. These are happy, talkative, fortunate. My fingers itch to touch the spines displayed across from me and I sense nooks I can't see, sturdy ladders that reach to the tops, and to my delight, a mezzanine that runs around two sides of the room. A skylight overhead illuminates more shelves of books up there and I am struck with awe.

"Yes, I promise. I'll see you at seven."

Leo appears from between two stacks. Today he is dressed in a long-sleeve button down shirt, and a vest with a pocket watch attached as he completes his Bluetooth call. He's headed for his desk before he realizes I'm there and pulls up short. He takes half a step back, as if startled. "Miss Sherwood?"

He's forgotten our meeting. It's evident in his face and the tone of surprise in his voice. "Good morning."

All around me, the volumes fall silent. The ends of my fingers tingle. I no longer feel sure of myself, but I wonder if it's from the magick coating this place or because Leo is so close.

"I didn't realize you were my first appointment," he says, regaining his composure. His beard is longer than when I saw him last month, his hair escaping the pomade he's used to tame it. Dark, expressive, green eyes dart to me and away, landing on Jayne. A frown tips the corners of his lips down behind the beard.

I rush to assure him I made one. "When I called last week, this was the time I was told to arrive."

"Of course." He stops at the desk and takes off the Bluetooth, dropping it near the phone. "I didn't realize you were interested in the position. I hate to break this to you, but you can't bring your dog to work."

"What? No, I'm not applying. I spoke to a woman, I assume your assistant, who told me I could bring several old books by to have you appraise them."

I swing the pack off and move toward a chair near him. Unzipping it, I begin pulling them out, and since there's no clean place to set them, I hold one out to him.

"You must have spoken to my *former* assistant. That's why I'm looking for a new curator." He doesn't take it from my hand, his gaze scanning it. "A simple mix-up, I guess."

His gaze returns to mine, a finger pointing to my items. "Where did you find these?"

"A secret chamber!" I step closer. "It's so amazing, we didn't realize the turret on our house actually contained a real room, and then we discovered it was full of our grandmother's books..."

The edition I'm still holding has become heavy in my hand and I hug it to me. Jayne sits a few feet away, her gaze on Leo. "I hate to part with them, but I was hoping a few might be worth money."

He goes to the top drawer and removes a pair of gloves, sliding them on. Reaching for the book I'm holding, he glowers at my dilapidated backpack. "Always treat old books with the greatest of care." It sounds as though he's chastising me. "You don't want the oils from your hands to damage the paper."

I bite my tongue and hand him the book. He seems curious as he reads the title, his gaze darting to mine and back before he opens it and begins to thumb through the contents. He pauses here and there to read a section, his face a mask of neutrality.

That surprises me. The book is definitely an odd one and contains magickal spells.

He lays it down on a stack on his desk and holds his fingers out for another. I hand the second to him, and he examines it with the same care. The third barely holds his attention, and he returns to the first one, that spellbinding gaze engulfing me again.

The Beastly Book of Spells describes magickal ceremonies, charms, and enchantments used to control wild animals to do a witch's bidding. It is handwritten, with no official publication date or other source listed. We've all questioned why my grandmother had such a guide in her possession, but she may have been the original witch in our family. Ruby has tried reaching out to her ghost, but she's not talking—at least as a spirit—and neither is the book itself.

I take a hesitant step forward, pointing at the title. "I saw what looked like a similar book downstairs in your sitting room."

He scans through the fragile pages. "Legend has it there was an outbreak of wild animals turning on Story Cove townsfolk in the early eighteen hundreds. It was always believed witches had something to do with it, but no one could prove it. It *is* similar, although it's more practical then metaphysical. This book may date to that time period, and with the handwritten notes in the margins, could add a new layer of evidence to what is now only mythical wives tales. I've been trying to link factual history to those stories, but I've come up dry."

He examines the binding, the back cover.

I feel excitement rising. "Do you think these have monetary value, then? That one in particular?"

He nods. "It's difficult to estimate the value of this book, but the others are probably worth fifty to seventy-five dollars apiece."

My heart sinks. That's barely a drop in the bucket for what we need. "Could that be more valuable, though?" I pointed at the one he was still holding.

"Hard to say. May I take pictures of it? I'll check with my contact who deals in magickal items. She may have an interest in it."

"You don't?"

His expression goes hard. "Perhaps."

He snaps a few pictures with his phone, and my nerves get the better of me. All of this and the best I may get isn't even two hundred dollars? "Take a wild guess. Do you think that's worth more than seventy-five?"

The phone buzzes on the desk and Albert's voice announces the applicant for the curator job has arrived.

Leo hands the book to me. "I'll be in touch as soon as I have more information."

"Of course. Thank you." He ushers Jayne and I to the elevator, and I quickly shove the books in the backpack and zip it up. He seems so stiff now, so formal.

"This position," I query as we wait for the elevator to open. I'm disappointed I didn't get to touch his books, share more of a conversation with him. "Does your assistant get the honor of taking care of your amazing collection?"

His sharp gaze flicks to me. "Yes, quite. I need someone with experience to manage my library, research and catalogue recent acquisitions, and perform light administrative duties."

The elevator dings and the doors open. Linda Longrove, the former Story Cove librarian, steps out. In a dark gray pantsuit and a large tote on her arm, she startles at seeing me.

Of all the people to get their hands on Leo's library...

"Why Belle." Recovering quickly, she's sugared charm. "I hope *you're* not the competition."

Her tone signifies I'm *no* competition, at least in her mind. I bite my tongue once again, leading Jayne into the elevator as if she's not even there. "I'll leave my number with your butler," I tell Leo with a forced smile.

The corner of his lips twitches so slightly I'm not sure I even saw them move, but I swear he's hiding a smile behind his thick beard.

After speaking to Albert, Jayne and I walk out, the beautiful day greeting us once again. "Linda is bad news," I declare.

Jayne never liked her either and snorts her agreement as we leave the veranda and step around the woman's tan hatchback in the drive.

She was disliked by everyone across the board who involved with the library. She was fired under suspicious circumstances after only working there a year.

As Jayne and I trek our way to Beanstalk Books, I debate telling Leo about her possible lack of professionalism but I barely know him. I'm not one to spread gossip, and yet, it eats at me, thinking about her smug attitude.

"The curator would be an ideal position for you," I hear Jayne's voice inside my head.

Glancing down, I see my witchy familiar and best friend grinning through her layers of muzzle hair. Her voice always sounds like a nightclub singer's, low and gravely. "Yes, it would," I agree out loud. "But I already have a job—two, in fact. Both of which I love. I hardly need another."

She stops to sniff at a dandelion, its white seeds ready to spread in the breeze. *"Neither of which come with an eccentric millionaire."*

A very handsome eccentric millionaire, to be exact.

"There is that," I say and giggle at the thought.

THREE

"We're nearly out of maps," Daisy exclaims as I walk through the door of Beanstalk Books after my daily stop to deposit Enchanted's profits from the previous day.

She and Jayne greet each other, and Jayne takes her special place in the front window on a large, red velvet pillow with gold trim.

Daisy and I have cleared a space near the mystery section for the signing on Saturday, and she's redone a display table beside it with a collection of the authors' coveted books. The latest release is selling like gang-busters and I've ordered extra copies from the publisher.

"I'll make more." I shrug off the backpack. The walk from Leo's cleared my head and I'm ready to get down to business. Excitement flutters in my chest as we prepare for the fair and I anticipate seeing several vendors who come from all over, bringing in assorted rare and out-of-print additions.

Daisy feels the excitement, too, her aging fingers moving quickly between her coffee cup, a stack of paperbacks we just got in, and the register. Various customers file in and out as the morning goes by and some of our sellers arrive early and visit the bookstore to sign in and pick-up a map.

My favorite is Augusta Pennyweather, known as the Book Peddler. She has a cute RV with a cartoon version of herself on the side that she travels in from town to town, selling her books.

The moment she walks in, she brings a new level of anticipation. Her curly red hair flies in all directions and her cowboy boots clomp on the hardwood floor. "Jayne, my sweetheart," she exclaims over the dog, stroking her ears and kissing the end of her nose.

Jayne wags her tail and hops onto all fours to climb into Augusta's lap when she sits in the sunny window with her.

"You made it," I say grabbing the clipboard and marking an X by her name. I hand her a map. "It's good to see you."

"Wouldn't be anywhere else this week. Hello, Daisy."

Daisy waves, sliding books into a bag for a customer. "Good to see you, Pennyweather."

Augusta and I catch up on what's been happening in both of our worlds for a few minutes as I dust one of the shelves and she continues to pet Jayne. "I finally tracked down one of those books in the series you collect."

My pulse skips. "Which title?"

"The third—the fairytale about the monster, and the young woman who saves him from a curse."

The Bewitching Harriet series is one my mother used to read to me growing up. I've been trying to track down the originals for years. I have three out of five and this one—*Harriet and the Magic Monster*—is special to me, as I always saw myself as the heroine. "I can't believe you found it."

"I went to an estate sale in North Dakota and there were numerous boxes of books. I offered to take the whole lot for a good price, and it wasn't until a few days ago that I was going through the last and discovered that story."

"Were there any others from the series?"

She shakes her head, eyes dancing as Jayne gets one of her toys. "I rechecked all of them, knowing you'd need confirmation the final book wasn't hidden in the group, but unfortunately, no. This one's a doozy though. You're going to love it."

I've been coveting this book since our mother died when I was a teen. I bite my lower lip, wondering how much Augusta will ask for it. On top of the expansion, and my dreams of buying this bookstore, it's another expense. Probably not a huge one, but still...it feels selfish to spend money on it.

The thing is, it's more than simply a book to me. Besides the fact it's rare—the whole series is extremely hard to find—it brings back memories of Mom. Cherished ones I covet as much as having a physical copy of it.

The one we had went missing around the time she and dad were killed in a car accident. I've searched the house and shop repeatedly and never been able to locate the third or fifth volumes in the series. I've thought of asking Leo to track them down for me, but I know he charges a fee for his services. I've been hoping Augusta would find it, since she loves a treasure hunt and doesn't charge anything for searching.

Augusta and Jayne play with the toy as I help Daisy with a rush of customers. One wants to locate a book we don't have in stock, so I place an online order for it. Another wants an entire series of hardbound cookbooks, and I gleefully ring them up and help her with the heavy stack.

Augusta folds up her fair map and sticks it in her back pocket, rolling the sleeves of her blue jean shirt to the elbow. "Time to set up. I've got a lot of unpacking to do."

"I'll be fine for a few minutes," Daisy says, waving me toward the door. "Go make sure everyone's playing nice over there."

Leaving with Augusta to get a view of the park where the vendors will be, I'm delighted to see several have pulled in to the parking lot. One looks confused about his spot, and I hurry over to check on him.

"I'm supposed to be there." He points to the prized corner location. "That's my slot."

"I had to rearrange several of the booths to accommodate some local crafters who are joining the fair this year," I explain.

The two in question—sisters who take old and damaged books and create art with them—have their tent already erected. I hand him a map and assure him his new location is even better, leading him to the chalk outline and pointing out the high traffic that will stream past as people come and go from the park itself. He eyes me with suspicion but the sisters offer to help him set up his tables and he seems mollified.

Across from us is the library, a small municipal parking lot, and a historic walking trail that winds through a wooded area and down to the old mill by the river. A handful of volunteers are setting up tables at both entrances to sell donated books and extra copies of those I've weeded from the shelves.

Molly Fitzgerald, the current librarian, tapes colorful banners with the various genres listed on the tables to aid buyers in their search. She walks with a cane, even though she's only thirty, but today, she's left it behind in her eagerness to assist the helpers. She's obsessed with Edgar Allen Poe, which is one of the reasons I like her, and she's much easier to get along with than Linda, although she can be stubborn about certain things.

One of the banners gets away from her on the breeze and I run to catch it. She limps toward me and smiles as I hand it to her. "Thanks."

Jayne visits as I help Molly secure the sign.

Everyone is in a jovial mood and the warm day adds to our happiness.

"Be sure to check with Gunther first thing," Molly tells me. He's one of the vendors close to our book-loving hearts who often donates boxes of paperbacks, claiming we're his favorite on the circuit. "He's supposed to have a new inventory of local history editions. We need to beef up our reference section, especially when it comes to that."

"Of course. I'll stop there before I go to the book-store. I also want to check with Tom to see if he found any rare and unique biographies."

The items in my backpack pop into my mind and I think about offering them, but Molly has a different perspective on things and doesn't like books she considers 'unhealthy' for people to read. She doesn't believe in or condone magick, even white magick like my sisters and I use.

With the library's limited budget, she steers away from romance novels and mainstream thrillers, and tends toward the history and nonfiction sections. She often quotes, "those who do not learn from history are doomed to repeat it."

I have to bite my tongue and not correct her with the original: "Those who cannot remember the past are condemned to repeat it." I figure it's not worth making an enemy over, and both mean basically the same thing.

More vendors arrive and begin setting up. The afternoon flies by and eventually, Jayne and I head back to help Daisy close. She's overdone it and is quite tired when I send her upstairs to her private quarters to rest.

As Jayne and I stand outside Enchanted, I hear conversation and laughter in the air. All day, various books have talked to me. I can't wait to return tomorrow and listen to their stories.

For now, I go inside and work on mine.

FOUR

The next day, I enjoy breakfast with my sisters and update them on Leo's assessment.

I can tell they're as disappointed as I am, but Cinder gives me a smile. She's pulled her hair into a knot on top of her head, securing it with a pencil. Zelle, my twin and our resident hair and makeup expert, chastised her about it, but she's doing renovations today and wants it out of her face. "Don't worry about selling those. They're part of our history, and our family is more important than the money for the shop."

This is true, but I hate that Cinder is bearing so much of the burden for the expansion, doing all the work herself. We're pinching every penny and it will be worth it in the end. We'll increase our line of body products and Zelle and I will get more hours here. As it is, we both have to work part-time at our other jobs to help pay bills. Our house is over two-hundred years old and the constant repairs on it alone keep us on a strict budget.

We're doing what we can to bring in extra funds. I need to contribute in some way. "I'm bringing them to the fair to see if one of the vendors might offer a higher price."

Zelle squeezes my shoulder. Her own hair is barely an inch long right now. By evening, it will be down to her ankles. She's tipped the ends a bright silver. "There's the Pollyanna we know and love."

I roll my eyes. "Hope costs nothing, as Mom always said, and I believe in magick and fairytales."

Our parents definitely had a fairytale marriage, and we add a touch of white magick to each batch of products.

"Me, too," Cinder says with a wink.

I counted my cash this morning and I'm hoping I have enough to buy *Harriet and the Magic Monster*. The money burns a hole in my pocket, not because I'm desperate to spend it, but I feel guilty for doing so.

I help Ruby clean up before I kiss her freckled cheek and journey next door to see Daisy. It's not quite opening time, and the elderly woman bustles around, happy business was up yesterday. Her thin white hair is flying in every direction, like an imitation of Einstein.

I give her a small sample of cream Cinder made last night for her arthritic joints. It contains a sprinkling of magick, along with mint and rosemary, to ease her pain. "Use some every two hours."

"I will," she assures me. "Now go check on the fair sellers. Augusta has that book for you. Get back here when you can."

From under the counter, I grab the blue zippered bag "First, I'll hit the bank and drop this off with our deposit."

"Thank you, dear."

I stash it in my backpack and heft it onto my shoulder. "Molly wants me to check on titles Gunther is supposed to have. Outside of the historical society members, no one checks out the collection the library already has on hand."

Daisy makes a dismissive noise. She understands my frustrations with Molly's limited perspective on what patrons want to read. "It's a snooze fest over at the library these days." She rubs the cream into her finger joints and sighs. "That place needs adventure stories! Murder mysteries! Romance!"

At this, she winks. I grin. "Couldn't agree more. Come on, Jayne. Let's go."

After the drop, we make the rounds to ensure the sellers have what they need. I'm greeted by most and offered coffee and assorted breakfast items. Everyone seems fairly happy with their locations, and there are only a few issues with signs and tent tie-downs that are easily resolved.

Gunther is peddling several local history books in excellent condition. They might be good additions, and I ask him to hold them for us. It's up to Molly to decide what she wants and how much she's willing to pay.

Jayne greets the regulars, acquiring a few nibbles of food herself from her favorites, before we journey to the library. Ronald, Molly's husband, greets me with a big smile. She's inside prepping for the day, and as the fair opens, several volunteers arrive to set up tables outside the front and side entrances, under Ronald's guidance.

I give a list of Gunther's titles to him to share with Molly. He adjusts his corduroy vest and slips it into a pocket. "I'll check with her and run over as soon as I can to buy what we can afford." He scratches Jayne behind the ear. "Mol was up a lot last night with her hip. I know she wants to walk around and look at the booths, so I hope it improves. I'm worried about her overdoing it."

"Her and Daisy both. I could bring her some of our joint cream," I offer.

"I'd appreciate it," he says, "but I doubt she'll use it. She's stubborn about it. She says she simply believes if she doesn't acknowledge it, it will go away."

Molly was in an accident years ago when a stray dog ran in front of her car on a deserted strip outside town, and her hip hasn't been right since. That's why she uses the cane, and I know some days are worse than others, even though she never complains.

Gossip says she might have been drunk, but charges were never filed. Either way, I feel bad for her to be hurting almost constantly. Books are her escape, like they are for so many, allowing us to enjoy not just one life, but many. They can contain daring adventures that take us away from everyday problems, allowing us to leave our pain-filled bodies and stressful situations.

I say goodbye and make my way to Augusta's booth. It's one of the more flamboyant, and she has quite a range of items, from older first editions to recent bestsellers.

As I step into her tent, I hear the murmur of dozens of volumes, all holding conversations with each other, and I feel tickled, like an eavesdropper, listening to their stories.

Augusta's helping another customer, so it gives me time to browse, and I see book after book I wish I could buy. Of course, my to-be-read pile is as high as the turret of our house, and I still have dozens of my great grandmother's journals to peruse. If I could lock myself away for months and delve into everything I want, I'd be a happy witch.

When she finishes, she turns to me with a glowing smile and claps. "I've got it back here."

She reaches behind the table holding her cash drawer and takes it out. The sight of it makes me suck in a breath.

Wrapped in plastic, it shimmers in the light. She holds the edition out and I take it reverently to examine it. The cover and spine are perfect.

A rush of emotion floods through me as memories

of my mother surface. This is it. The book I've been searching for.

"Not a mark on it," Augusta tells me. "It's in amazing shape. I'm not sure anyone has ever read it."

The perfect 'used' copy—*like new.*

I swallow the tightness in my throat and lift my gaze to hers. "How much?"

"Don't you want to take it out and get a better look at it?"

The backpack on my shoulder feels heavier. With trembling fingers, I do as she suggests and remove it carefully from the protected plastic, thinking of Leo's reprimand yesterday. I stroke the title and gently open the cover.

Just like with the copy I remember, the edges of the pages have gold on them, each chapter beginning with a beautiful picture.

"It's amazing." I bite my lip, feeling my eyes tear. The book makes a purring noise as if enjoying my fingers flipping lightly through the pages. "It's perfect. I can't believe you found one in such good shape."

"I can't either, to be honest. When you told me how old that set was, especially since they weren't widely known, I knew it was going to take a bunch of luck to find them."

Glancing up again, I push through my nerves to repeat the important question. "How much do you want for it, Augusta?"

"Honey, you know I did my research. A rare book like this in good condition can be valuable. What makes it even more so is the fact it's signed and dated by the author."

My heart leaps. A signed copy! But then it sinks just as fast. Sure enough, I flip back to the beginning and see the autograph on the title page. The value is rising by the moment. "Oh, my goodness. That's incredible."

"I spoke to another buyer who's interested and willing to pay three hundred."

I only have seventy-five in my pocket. Most of the time, that would buy a dozen old books. My heart falls into my stomach and my shaking fingers close the book. I fight the disappointment as I return it to the plastic wrapper. "I'm afraid that's way out of my range."

Augusta accepts the book with reluctance. "For you, I'm willing to offer a discount. How about two?"

That's still more than I was prepared to pay. I try not to let my sadness show and offer her a smile. "You have to make money, too."

"Like I told you, I got a good deal on the whole lot, and if I sell a bunch of them this week at the fair, I'll make my investment back, as well as enough to make rent."

I shift my weight back and forth. What should I do? "Would you be interested in a trade? I have a couple of books that belonged to my fourth great-grandmother. Very old and rare. I'd be willing to part with them if you're interested."

"A barter?'

I nod. "I have some cash, but maybe you know a buyer who'd want them and we could trade for what I don't have?"

"Sure. What'd'ya got?"

I show her the three volumes, but her face screws up as she looks at them. She thumbs through the odd book of spells and shakes her head. "I'm sorry, hun, but the best I can do is seventy-five for the lot."

My hopes plummet. Both of us dance around the amount, but in the end, I decide to keep the books, hoping against hope I can get more from Leo's contact.

"I sure hate to let this go to anyone else," Augusta says, running a respectful finger over the plastic wrap. "No telling if I'll find another, and surely not one in this shape."

The side flap of the tent is up and next to Augusta is a vendor named Bobby Dean Sutton. He's been eavesdropping and saunters in, thumbs hooked in his belt loops. "I'll give you a hundred dollars for that set," he declares.

It's not enough, but I'm tempted. Even that leaves me nothing for the expansion fund and still short of what I should pay Augusta.

Bobby Dean is disliked by many of the others and nearly always ends up in a quarrel over the price of his books with folks. I avoid him, since he rubs me the wrong way every time I encounter him. "I think I'll hang onto them for now, but thank you."

"Your loss," he grumbles.

As Augusta tucks the book away, Linda strolls up.

Bobby Dean returns to his booth and the two strike up a conversation. They know each other from previous fairs.

"I'm sorry," I say to Augusta.

"Now don't you worry about it." She waves me off. "I'm sorry I can't just give it to you."

Bobby Dean and Linda burst out laughing, and Augusta and I exchange an eyeroll.

Graham Geyer, one of my favorite library patrons, is examining a book in Bobby Dean's booth. He raises it in greeting as I'm leaving Augusta's, and I see it's an old Steinbeck novel. Not rare or unique, but I know Mr. Geyer is sentimental about books from his childhood, like I am, and it's probably one of them.

Before I get a foot past the booth, Mr. Geyer offers ten dollars for it and Bobby Dean refuses with a sneer. "Don't be a cheapskate. That's a classic! Fifteen."

"A classic that's on eBay for half that," Geyer counters. "I'll give you seven."

Bobby Dean narrows his eyes. "Then buy it off the internet. I hope you get scammed!"

Mr. Geyer sets the book down with a thump and stomps off.

Linda, watching the interaction, shakes her head. "You don't need that grumpy old coot's business."

The two of them return to flirting.

"Jayne?" The dog is missing. I double back to Augusta's, finding my familiar laying at her feet. "Come on, girl. We need to check on Daisy."

As I lean over to clip the leash on her collar,

Augusta whispers in my ear. "He's worse than ever. Refuses to negotiate with anyone."

I bend down so Bobby Dean and Linda can't see me. Jayne licks my hand. "I have to find a way to un-invite him next year."

She nods in agreement. "In the last town, he got into it with a young kid over a set of comic books. Can you believe it?"

I straighten and eye the other booth. They're discussing a book Linda's holding. "I'm sorry you have to be next to him."

Augusta turns her back on them and pretends to sort a stack of thrillers behind her on the shelf. I hear them pleading for me to buy them. "Those comics weren't worth the price of a bad coffee. The whole incident upset the kid's folks so much they came to the fair and got into it with him. The father and Bobby Dean ended up in a fist fight."

"You're kidding! Well, he better behave himself here or the town council will toss him out on his ear."

Augusta and I exchange a look, both half hoping for such an incident.

Later that afternoon, I take a break from Beanstalk Books and wander to the library to see how the volunteer sales are going. Molly is outside talking to several patrons.

"I sent Ronald to buy two from that list," she tells me, breaking away, "but I'm hoping to get over there myself and see what else we might purchase for the stacks." She leans closer and lowers her voice.

"Of course, I want to see what I can buy for myself, too."

We share a chuckle, and I wish I could be more excited about the prospect. I think about *Harriet and the Magic Monster* and the two-hundred dollars. There has to be something I can sell in my collection to raise that money.

"Just avoid Bobby Dean Sutton," I advise. "He's being his usual annoying self and already got into it with Mr. Geyer, of all people."

Molly shakes her head, frowning. "I don't like to speak ill of anyone, but the event would be better without the likes of him. You should revoke his invite."

Before Jayne and I return to the bookstore, I run inside Enchanted. Ruby looks up surprised from behind the register. "Home already?"

"I have an idea about some of Eunice's books—remember there were several in Latin that none of us can read? I'm taking them to the fair and see if any of the vendors are interested. I was thinking about Gunther and his history books. I believe he knows Latin."

Ruby smiles and tucks a strand of her dark hair behind an ear. "Good idea."

In the secret room, I gather the volumes from a lower shelf and dust them off. They're talking to me, but I don't understand a word.

As I add them to my backpack, I ask Eunice's blessing in selling them. "I really need some money," I say, "and your books need a good home."

We eat a late dinner, our Uncle Odin and godmother, Matilda, joining us. Cinder has been working on the beginnings of our remodeling project and is full of details about reconstructing a partial wall. My mind wanders and I play with my food, earning Ruby's annoyance.

"Don't you like it?" She points to the pumpkin soup and cornbread.

"It's delicious." I slurp soup and nibble a piece to reassure her.

Across the table, Zelle, gives me the stink eye. "Your awfully distracted. Is Daisy okay?"

I sip my warm chai tea and nod. "Business is up, and everyone is excited about the reading this weekend. Tomorrow is our official kick off and all the vendors have arrived."

"And how is Mr. Kingsley?" Matilda asks. Our

godmother is sporting a sequined dress, completely over the top for our informal family dinner. A former Valkyrie, she's an interesting character and finds plenty of trouble to get into. It's a signal she's going out after we're through, but she's very secretive about what she's been doing lately in the evenings.

"He's fine," I tell her, explaining about his appraisal. "I'm going to continue sorting through as many as I can and see if I can sell some at the fair. I'm also searching the attic to see if there are any antiques we could sell, like Nonni did to Mr. Kingsley. If any of you have time, I'd appreciate help."

Uncle Odin adjusts his eye patch and picks up his spoon. "I would be happy to assist, my dear."

Zelle finishes and wipes her fingers on her napkin. "Just don't sell anything I want to keep."

Next to her, Matilda nods. "And don't touch my stuff. I stowed some of it in the back room, and I might need it one of these days."

Cinder gives her a wary look. "Like when? Are you planning on moving out?"

Matilda sticks out her tongue good-naturedly. "Hey, you never know. You guys are doing great on your own, and if I do, I'll be close by."

Ruby won't let me help clean up, shooing me off to hunt. Zelle goes with me. For the next hour, we come up with a couple of antique tables, and then we head to the tower to sort through books. My twin's hair is in a braid that hangs all the way to her ankles. This week she's changed her highlights to a beautiful bright apricot in keeping with the fall season. Pumpkin colored low lights accent those and the braid is a beautiful piece of artwork.

I hate that she has to shave her hair every morning and start over, but if she doesn't, she will be completely wrapped up in it, and the weight will pull so hard on her scalp she'll barely be able to drag herself around.

The good thing is she loves coloring and styling it, and her magick allows her to change it anytime she wants.

She locates a book in a language neither of us recognize. It's not Latin, not French, and we're both stumped, so Zelle puts it aside with our stack of potentials. By the time we haul them downstairs, it's close to ten.

Cinder is pouring candles and Ruby is labeling them. I'm exhausted, but I have an idea and share it with my sisters. "Tomorrow, I'm putting a table next door for a sidewalk sale. Why don't we do the same with our products? We could do a fall display with the apple and pumpkin candles, maybe a second with various soaps."

"I love that," Cinder says. "Where are the old card tables?"

"In the back." Zelle hops on the counter and shows them the volume we can't decipher. "I'll pull them out tonight and clean them up. Do either of you recognize this language?"

Ruby takes the book and thumbs through it, shaking her head. "I could Google it."

Cinder goes to work on scrubbing the aluminum pot. "Do you think it's valuable?"

I shrug. "I can't understand what it's saying to me, but it feels like it has magick woven into the words."

Ruby finishes labeling and stands, shoving her stool away and stretching. "Check with Uncle Odin and Matilda. They might have an idea if it's from the old country."

It's a good idea. Zelle and I exchange a look. "I'll take it to Matilda."

She climbs the stairs and I wonder if it's too late to call Leo. Surely he's had time to talk to his contact by now.

I carry the magickal guide to the front counter and place it next to my backpack so I won't forget it in the morning. I take out the spell book and fiddle with it, reading through a few incantations. They make my stomach turn. Why would anyone want to control a wild animal and put it under thrall?

Shuddering, I place it on the other and return to the work area. "Do you need help gathering products?" I ask my remaining sisters.

Cinder and Ruby tell me no, and I leave them to it, going to my bedroom on the second floor. I stare at my phone for several minutes, debating whether it's rude, but I figure if Leo's in bed, Albert will answer.

As I'm dialing, I feel my pulse speed up. I realize

it's not the hour that makes me nervous. It's talking to him in general.

Why do I feel this way? He's not at all my type outside of his amazing library, and he's given me no reason to think he's interested in me. Of course, my sisters and godmother see it differently and like to tease me about him.

It's silly, because the most interaction we've had was at Ms. Starling's dinner, and that was pretty minimal.

As the call goes through, I hold my breath. *Please let it be Albert,* I think in sudden panic.

"Mr. Kingsley's residence," the butler's voice announces promptly when he picks up on the second ring. "May I help you?"

I release my breath slowly, pulse hammering in my ears "Albert, sorry to bother you so late. It's Belle Sherwood, from the soap shop? Leo was going to check with one of his contacts. Is it possible he's still awake?"

There's a hesitant pause. "Let me check, Miss."

I'm put on hold, and it takes forever. I almost hang up, wondering if he even went to get Leo, or if Leo's just taking his sweet time to answer.

"Miss Sherwood." Leo's deep voice reverberates through my entire body, sending warm chills down my spine. "What can I help you with?"

All thoughts skitter out of my head. "I'm.. You... I mean..." I beat the heel of my hand against my forehead. *Come on, Belle! Get it together!*

I clear my throat and try again. *No man leaves me speechless.* "I'm truly sorry to bother you this late, Mr. Kingsley. I was hoping you might have news regarding the book I showed you. Were you able to speak to your contact about it?"

Annoyance laces his voice. "My days are busy and I was not able to make that call. I will contact Raven tomorrow."

His tone tells me he doesn't appreciate my impatience. "That would be great. I really need to know if the book is worth anything while the fair is in town."

"And why is that?"

I don't want to tell him about *Harriet and the Magic Monster* or explain our financial situation due to the expansion. "I may have someone else who's interested," I tell him. I have no intention of selling the book to Bobby Dean, but he doesn't need to know that. "Please let me know as soon as possible if your buyer is as well."

The annoyance in his voice fades, but testiness takes its place. "I'll get back to you in the morning. Is that soon enough?"

At least he understands I'm not sitting on my hands waiting for him. "First thing would be excellent. Talk to you then."

I disconnect, heart still thumping, and eye my laptop where my romance novel waits for me to write the next lines. The familiar sounds of my sisters downstairs is comforting, and I run my fingers along the edge of the case, a new scene popping into my head.

I'm about to open it and start writing when Zelle stops in the doorway. "Matilda doesn't recognize it either."

I whirl, shielding the laptop and acting nonchalant. My writing labors are not ready for the public yet. "Think we should sell it?"

A shrug as she touches the spine. "Uncle Odin can research it, if you want. You'll have to remind him, though. You know how forgetful he is."

This is quite a puzzle if Matilda has no clue. "Could you put it downstairs near the register with the others? I'll take it tomorrow and ask around while he's doing that. Feel a few of the vendors out, maybe show it to Leo. Surely, someone will know what it's about and how much it's worth."

After she leaves, Jayne and I climb into bed. I'm exhausted and tomorrow is another day full of selling books, helping my sisters, and running the fair. My novel will have to wait.

I'm dreaming I'm dancing in Leo's library when a loud crash wakes me. I bolt upright, mind fuzzy from the dream and chest heaving as if I've run a mile.

Jayne barks and dashes to the floor. I rub my eyes and follow as she flies down the steps. My sisters call out, asking what the noise was.

As I flip on lights and hurry through the first floor, I feel a cool breeze on my feet and arms, and hear the too-loud sound of frogs and crickets.

Swinging through the work room, I pull up short. One of the front display windows has been shattered, the outside street lamp illuminating a dirty brick lying on the floor with dozens of glass shards around it reflecting the light.

A book is on the floor, too, near the counter, but nothing else seems disturbed. The fall showcase of apple scented soaps and lotions is intact, although covered in glass. Behind it, the antique table with an arrangement of pumpkin spice candles in all sizes is also unharmed.

"Oh no," Zelle says, rushing in and pulling up short in her bare feet. "What in the world?"

As Jayne starts sniffing, I wrap a bubble of magick around her to protect her paws. The others follow, staring in shock. My skin tingles, the cool night air raising the tiny hair on my arms.

Or perhaps it's the magick I sense floating in here that causes the reaction. It's so faint, I can barely detect it, and seems to be emanating from the brick.

"What did they steal?" Cinder asks, her eyes scanning the shop and taking inventory.

"I don't think they stole anything," I assure her as I shoo Jayne away and survey the brick. The grimy, dull rust colored bar is heavy. I dust it with magick, but the ethereal traces causing my skin to tingle disappear like invisible strands into the night. I can't get a read on them. "It must have just been vandalism. Probably kids."

She waves a hand, her magick reaching out to count the products, just to be sure. Ruby grabs a pan and broom and begins sweeping as Zelle cautiously gathers the biggest pieces and tosses them in the trash.

As I carefully navigate my way through the damage and pick up the book from the floor, I realize I may be wrong about the thievery.

The Beastly Book of Spells is gone.

CHAPTER

SIX

Our cousin, Robyn Wood, is a detective for the Story Cove Police Department. She responds to my call, bringing several officers with her.

I'm shaken and questioning the fact that someone would break in to steal the book. Matilda puts out the SOS and our family circles their magickal wagons. Our grandparents, Nonni and Poppi, bring Snow and her watchdog and familiar, Runa, a large, white wolf-hybrid who Jayne adores. Along with them, Cinder's boyfriend, Finn Starling, arrives, bringing his movie-star good looks and competent air.

"You're sure there's nothing else missing?" Robyn queries, a compact blue notebook in hand. "They didn't make off with cash from the register or charge card receipts?"

The store feels crowded with all of us in it. "It wasn't disturbed. Even if that's what they were after, they would have come up empty-handed. I clear it out at closing every evening and place the cash and receipts in the safe. I take the whole lot to the bank the next day."

I worry my bottom lip as she records the information. "Tell me exactly what you heard and did."

"I was sleeping and there was a loud crash. Jayne and I ran down here. She was barking, so maybe she scared off whoever it was and they didn't have time to take anything else."

Robyn's face turns pensive. "Why steal a novel? Is there something special about it?"

"Not a novel. More of a..."

"Handbook," Zelle supplies. "A guide of sorts."

"About what?" Robyn asks.

My twin doesn't miss a beat. "Witchcraft."

Robyn stiffens.

I give her the title and explain that it came from our grandmother's hidden stash. Unfortunately, the other book with it, the one none of us understands, can't tell me anything.

"*The Beastly Book of Spells*?" Robyn echoes as she writes it in her pad. "I probably don't want to know what she used that for, do I?"

"No," Matilda answers, stroking Savannah's fur. "It was black magick."

Robyn's jaw tightens and she adds another note.

Zelle puts an arm around my waist and gives me a covert hug. "Maybe it was kids, like Belle said, and one simply dared his friend to run in and grab something."

Robyn screws up her face, her eyes tracing the route from the window to the counter and back to the sidewalk. "I suppose. Seems like they would have grabbed an item closer to the escape route, especially if he or she heard the dog raise the alarm."

"Everyone in town knows we live upstairs," Matilda interjects. "They'd be idiots to try and steal from us in such a blatant, noisy, manner."

Finn's gaze follows the same trajectory as Robyn's, as if he can envision the culprit busting the window and running for the counter. "I have to agree it resembles a random case of vandalism, but I see your point, Detective Wood. It's an odd and quite specific item to steal."

Jayne continues to sniff at the brick until one of the officers places it in an evidence bag. As Cinder uses her flexible tape measure on the window, Finn gives my elbow a squeeze. "The important thing is that you're all okay."

"Agreed," Snow says. She and Ruby are brushing tiny glass slivers from the pumpkin spice candles. As always, her jet black hair is perfectly coiffed and her beautiful eyes and porcelain skin captivate the male officers with Robyn.

Finn assists Cinder, and Robyn snaps her fingers at one of the cops. The poor guy is blatantly staring at Snow and jumps at being caught. "Get back to work."

He blushes, clears his throat, and fiddles with a yellow plastic marker on the floor.

"What kind of value did it have?" Robyn asks me.

"Not much." The fading adrenaline is draining my energy along with it. "Leo Kingsley appraised it yesterday. He was unsure, but indicated it's worth less than a hundred dollars. He stated he has an out-of-town buyer who might be interested, but he was in no hurry to contact her. I'm guessing it's not worth much more than the other books I showed him. This one is more unique, but..." I shrug.

"He knew you had this book?" She writes, suspicion clear in her voice.

I think about the trace magick on the brick and feel my stomach plummet. I can barely get the word out. "Yes."

"Who else?"

I think back over the previous day. "Augusta Pennyweather and Bobby Dean Sutton. I had it at the fair and showed it to them. Why?"

"Would either have reason to take it?"

"Robyn! You know Augusta. She would never steal a book—or anything else—from us!"

Robyn reserves comment. "And Mr. Sutton?"

I tap a finger against my arm. I'd love to blame this on him, but I keep thinking about the lingering magick. "Bobby Dean did offer to buy it."

Robyn writes down their names. "And Mr. Kingsley?"

"What about him?"

Zelle's arm tightens around my waist. "You can't be insinuating that he'd break in to rob us of a book worth so little?"

Robyn closes her notebook and gives us a tired, half-hearted smile. "I'll question all of them and see if anything turns up."

"Leo could just buy it." I step away from Zelle and follow Robyn to the door. "He has no reason to steal anything."

Her face is neutral with controlled patience. "Well someone did." She scans the shop. "All of these products, and the thief—who could have nabbed any of them—specifically took an old book. One we believe is rare but seemingly has negligible value…"

Snow comes up beside her. "Little value to normal people."

Her gaze meets each of ours as everyone stops what they're doing and stares at her.

"What are you suggesting?" Matilda asks.

"It's a spell book," Cinder states as if reading Snow's mind. "Witches use spell books."

Snow nods. "It may be of enormous value to one who wants to utilize those incantations."

"To control *beasts*?" Robyn barely spits out the last word.

"Animals, yes," Snow says. "Probably wild."

Zelle and I exchange a worried look. Cinder and Ruby join us, Ruby rubbing her arms from the chilly night air. "You think someone wanted the book in order to possess wild animals and use them for…what?"

Robyn's officers stop what they're doing and glance at her. She blanches slightly. "I don't know, but

I'll get back to you as soon as I've talked to those on the suspect list."

As if summoned, Leo appears on the sidewalk outside. He's dressed immaculately in black trousers, a white shirt, and a black wool jacket. His face is grim. "Miss Sherwood?" He marches through the door, nodding at Finn. "Are you all right?"

Robyn stares at me with a raised brow before addressing him. "Mr. Kingsley, we were just talking about you."

He ignores her, striding straight to me. His gaze scans me from head to toe. "Are you injured?"

A sudden rush of warmth fills my chest as his green gaze bores into mine. "We're all fine, thank you."

Savannah comes to her feet, meowing loudly. He turns his focus back to Finn. "What happened to the window?"

He and Finn struck up an interesting friendship when Finn's mother moved next door on Millionaires Row. "Someone busted it, ran inside, and grabbed a book from the counter." He points to the register where the other still sits. I hear it speaking, the voice deep and ancient, but the words make no sense.

Leo's intense gaze returns to mine. He gently takes my hand and a new warmth spreads rapidly through my body. "Which one?"

I search his face for subterfuge. Robyn's correct—there are only a few who knew about it, and whoever broke in went right for it.

"How did you hear about the break-in?" Robyn queries before I can answer.

His lips thin beneath his beard, and his focus doesn't leave my face as he responds. "Albert Franks, my butler. He heard it on the police scanner app he listens to."

Drowning in Leo's beautiful face, I wish I could hang onto him forever. "It was *The Beastly Book of Spells.* Only you and two others knew we had it."

Robyn flips open her notebook. "Which is why you and I are going to have a little conversation outside," she tells him.

His eyes harden and his attention ping-pongs between us before stopping on me. "You think *I* did this?"

Robyn motions him to follow her. "This way, Mr. Kingsley."

I feel sick to my stomach. Zelle, so connected to me, feels it, too. She rubs her belly, but manages to hang onto me when I start after them. "There's no way he had anything to do with this," I murmur.

All of my sisters offer supportive replies. Snow kisses my cheek and says goodnight. The two officers exit after her and hover near the police cruiser parked at the curb.

Finn, looking like a thundercloud about the situation, tells Cinder he'll get plywood from her remodeling stash out back to close the window for the rest of the night.

Matilda squeezes my hand and Uncle Odin gives

me a hug before they head upstairs. Ruby and Cinder leave to grab tools from the work room to help Finn.

I edge closer to the doorway to eavesdrop on Robyn's conversation with Leo, Zelle forced to come with me. As we try to blend into the wall and stay out of Robyn's line of sight, Savannah rubs against my ankles and Jayne sits in the doorway, unconcerned my cousin might see her.

"I was in bed," Leo claims. "You can ask Albert."

She scribbles. "Did Mr. Franks have any contact with this book?"

His voice is nearly a growl. "Not that I'm aware."

"Was he present when Belle showed them to you to appraise?"

"No. He sent her in the elevator, but Miss Sherwood had them in a backpack, and he remained downstairs. Besides, he has no interest in books like that one."

Robyn lifts her face and gives Leo a questioning perusal. "And why is that?"

Leo stares back confidently. "My butler doesn't believe in things like witchcraft. If he did, I have quite a collection of similar books."

"But this one is rare, I understand."

"If he wanted it, I would have gladly purchased it for him. I buy him books all the time."

"Is that so? This collection of magical editions you own, I'd like to see it tomorrow. I'll swing by around nine."

Leo tilts his head slightly. "You're interested in witchcraft?"

I know from experience that magick makes Robyn nervous. She's feigning interest in order to get inside his house, probably to speak to Albert or look for clues.

My cousin easily dodges the question. "Is there anyone else you've spoken to or who might have been at your home and knows about or saw Belle with it?"

He starts to say no, then stops himself. "Late tonight I contacted a buyer several towns away who deals specifically in metaphysical items. I mentioned the volume to her, and she expressed interest in it."

Robyn goes back to her pad. "I'll need her name and phone number."

"She's no criminal, detective."

A patient smile surfaces. "That's for me to decide."

Leo purses his lips before he reels off his contact's information. Seeming to restrain himself, he agrees that Robyn can see his collection. He doesn't offer any resistance to another set of questions, and I'm grateful.

After Robyn leaves, Leo steps inside to find me again. Savannah gloms onto him, rubbing his leg and purring as if she's discovered her long-lost friend. He gives her an absentminded pat as Finn returns with a large, cumbersome piece of plywood.

"I'll have a repair man here first thing in the morning." he assures me.

"Thank you, but really, that's not necessary."

Cinder straps on her toolbelt as she and Ruby haul

in boxes of screws and a couple of cordless screw-drivers. "We can handle it," she assures him.

Disappointment clouds his face. "I insist."

"Cinder's the best carpenter around," Finn tells him, grunting as he helps her wiggle the plywood into the open window. "She can fix it."

Leo steps up to add his own weight and support and it slides into place, blocking the view to the sidewalk.

"Plus, she works for free," I add.

My attempt at humor doesn't work and Leo gives me a nod, but seems hurt. I'm not sure if it's over our refusal of his assistance or the fact he's a suspect.

Once it's secured, everyone says goodnight. I wave as Leo drives toward the hill, and Ruby brings me a cup of chamomile.

Back in bed, I can't sleep. At my desk, I struggle to type the next scene in my romance, but my imagination won't cooperate. I keep thinking about the break-in, Leo, and the odd magick handbook still downstairs.

Giving up, I pull out a mystery, the fifth addition in the Benning's series, and climb into my window seat with Jayne.

I wrap a soft afghan around us as I attempt to escape into the fictional story, but my mind continually wanders. I end up re-reading the same chapter twice.

An hour later, I catch myself staring toward Leo's, my mind and heart drifting away to a dreamy dance in his library once more.

CHAPTER

SEVEN

Six am comes early when Savannah—better than any alarm clock—wakes me by howling in my face for her breakfast.

Jayne joins in, doing a funny version of whines and barks that sound like she's talking, while in actuality, she is, at least inside my head. "Hurry, hurry, hurry," she says, and as I ready myself for work, I tease them both about starving, since we *never* feed them.

Savannah acts haughty but is vocally demanding as we head to the kitchen. As I watch her waddle, her body shaped like a barrel about to burst, I mentally mention to Jayne she could stand to lose a few pounds.

"I heard that," Savannah snarls in my head.

I pause, having never heard her voice before. "Sorry," I apologize, "but it would be better for your health to watch your weight."

At the door, she turns, narrows her eyes, and wrinkles her nose at me. Once, twice, three times. If she were a witch, I'd be worried she just hexed me.

After feeding them, I grab a slice of homemade bread, perfectly toasted, thanks to Ruby—the best cook in the county—along with a cup of tea and a few apple slices, before heading downstairs.

The grouping of a few antiques from the attic stand stoically near the work table. My heart sinks thinking about selling them, but surely they're worth more than Eunice's books.

Ruby is trying to strengthen her psychic connection with our late grandmother, and I saw the way she touched several of the pieces last night. She enjoys having these personal items that belonged to generations of Sherwoods, and I know she hates to let them go just like I do the books.

The sight of the broken window, though now covered, is disheartening, throwing the shop's normal brightness into shadows. The display window that's still intact on the other side of the door lets in some sunshine and Savannah climbs onto the low sill to sun herself while she cleans her paws.

I stick the cash from the safe in the drawer and clear the register so it's ready. Cinder comes in and hugs me. "Did you get any sleep?"

"Not much."

"Ruby and I can handle the shop today. I know you have a lot to do. I'll send the deposit with Matilda."

"Thank you." Having one less job on my plate this morning is appreciated, but I see the concern in her eyes, and I try to relieve it. "I'm going to make the rounds at the fair before I check in with Daisy, then I'll be back. Let's set up the table for the sidewalk sale. The broken window stinks, but I bet the news is all over town and that will bring in the nosy busybodies. Maybe they'll buy lots of products!"

Cinder smiles at my positive thinking and waves her fingers around, releasing a magnetism charm. Tiny sparkles land on various products, and the magick will call to those who need the items to help in assorted ways, such as relieving stress, finding love, and manifesting better health. "Sounds good to me."

Together we haul two folding tables outside, and Uncle Odin brings a sandwich board sign. Cinder tells him to list a ten-percent-off sale on Apple Crisp scented products.

He makes several gestures with his fingers and mumbles something under his breath. Handwriting appears with a set of runes drawn on the top and bottom. He smiles, satisfied. "That should do it."

"Don't forget to research the language in that book," I remind him.

He gives me a quick salute. "I'll stop at Daisy's later and help if you need it."

"We'll be too busy," Matilda claims, strutting out the door. She's got the bank bag in hand. Her hair is a bright fuchsia shade and it matches her long, flowing skirt. She winks at me as she whisks by. "Stay safe, Belle."

Cinder and I exchange a look, wondering if Matilda's sixth sense is the cause of her proclamation or too much of her 'magick potion.'

Uncle Odin and Cinder return inside and Jayne and I set off for the fairgrounds. It's officially opening day, and I push aside thoughts about the stolen item, the broken window, and Leo. I have work to do and people and books to take care of.

It's the perfect weather to make people think of apple pie and pumpkin lattes, sunny and in the low sixties with a light breeze. I did a spell last week, asking the weather gods to bless the fair with exactly these types of conditions. I need to remember to make an offering in the woods to thank them.

The vendors are rolling up tent flaps and removing tarps to reveal their assortment of products. Some carry bookmarks and other related items, as well as the volumes of reading material. Laughter and good-natured chatter echoes through the park as early buyers, desperate to get the best deals before anyone else, begin to cluster in.

Leaves scatter across the parking lot and side-walks. I wish everyone good luck on their sales and double check the sign near the entrance directing people.

One of the knots holding the right side is loose so I re-tie it. Augusta isn't at her booth yet, and I think I'm going to miss her before I head to the bookstore. But as Jayne and I make one more round, she comes hustling in carrying a plastic tub full of her wares.

"Good morning," I call.

She gives a half-hearted wave, setting down the container and opening her booth. As I make my way over, she rolls up the front side, and I duck in. "Are you ready for today?"

She avoids my eyes as she reaches for the tub. "Yes, although I'm apparently under suspicion for breaking into your shop last night."

Oh boy, Robyn's already contacted her. "I'm sorry about that. Someone stole one of the books I showed you yesterday."

She glances up as she withdraws a set of best-selling novels and sets them on the table. "Are you all right? Did they take anything else?"

Jayne puts her nose in the air as if she can smell the paper and ink. I try to tune out the voices I hear coming from the stack. "Everyone is fine, and nothing else was stolen, which in and of itself is suspicious, I guess. Could be a simple case of vandalism. I know you didn't steal it, but the list of those who knew we had it are short. It's definitely weird."

She frowns, beginning to file the new books in with some she already has displayed. "Why would anyone want to steal one of them?"

Best not to mention a witch might be behind the situation. "Seems extreme, doesn't it?"

"Are you sure that's what they were really after?"

"It appears so."

She gives Jayne a pat, then resumes her unpacking. "I'm just glad you're all okay."

Leo hasn't called yet and I feel a bit antsy. "I hate

to ask a favor, but could you hang on to the Harriet book for the rest of the day? I'm trying to find a way to come up with the money, but I need more time."

She gives me a quick nod. "I guess I can do that."

"Thank you. Good luck with sales today."

Jayne leads me away, and I check my phone. Still nothing. Bobby Dean is still not as his booth and I wonder if Robyn is talking to him.

Maybe they've discovered he's the culprit. As I leave, I call her, but she assures me she hasn't made any arrests. "Mr. Sutton has an alibi. He was at Homer's bar on the edge of town and several people saw him. I'm following up with them and the bartender shortly."

So why isn't he here? Disconnecting, I notice I have twenty minutes before the bookstore opens. Maybe Bobby Dean is hungover, and if he is, it's just another reason for me to consider kicking him out .

He camps down by the river under the bridge every year, so I take the trail through the park and head there.

It's a peaceful walk, and we pass a few folks, Jayne enjoying the field trip. Birds sing overhead and squirrels dart in and out of trees, gathering nuts for the winter.

The paved trail becomes a dirt path and we wind our way toward the water, hearing it sluice over rocks along the banks. I spot Bobby Dean's truck and camper on the other end, and Jayne and I cross a swath of rocks to get to it.

As we near, my skin tingles and the tiny hairs on my arms rise under my jacket.

Something's wrong. I feel it even before I notice broken glass on the passenger side.

I stop Jayne and glance around. "Bobby Dean?"

My voice echoes off the trees, the sky above a bright blue that reflects in the water. Inching closer, I call again. "It's Belle Sherwood. Are you here?"

Dread weighs heavy in my stomach as if I've eaten one of the large river rocks. The birds fall silent, and there are no squirrels or forest creatures moving here.

Jayne growls low in her throat, staring at the truck. Her hackles stand.

"Stay," I command. Picking my way over the unstable rocks, I advance toward the driver's seat. The window has definitely been broken and there's blood on one of the jagged edges jutting up from the casement.

An odor hangs in the air, rank and metallic. The inside of the cab is shadowed, but the distinct form of a body slouched toward the passenger seat is evident. Blood is splattered on the seat, the steering wheel, the back window.

I recoil, the scent of blood everywhere. As my eyes adjust to the dim gloom, I suck in a breath. Ragged gashes cover his face, his clothes are in shreds, and his hands...

I have to step back and retch. Tears spill from my eyes.

His fingers are gone.

More than that, the stench of magick claws at me... it's dark and ugly, hanging in the air near the body.

My legs tremble. A shaft of sunlight ripples over the rocks as the breeze blows, and Jayne quietly sits beside me. I feel her strength flood into me and soon I can stand again. Swiping away the tears, I take several deep breaths and stare at the water. With shaking hands, I grab my phone once more and call Robyn.

"You need to get down to the river," I tell her.

"Belle? What's up? You sound weird."

"Just please hurry, Robyn."

Her voice switches to active concern. "What's happened now?"

I choke on the words, clear my throat, and try again. "It's Bobby Dean." There can be no doubt from what I've seen, but saying it is still nearly impossible. "He's...dead."

The thing I don't tell my cousin before she hangs up is that I'm quite sure the rips and gashes all over his face and body are teeth marks from a wild animal.

CHAPTER

EIGHT

"Looks like a bear attack." The area is taped off and Robyn is supervising as several officers snap pictures and gather evidence. One is from last night and he nods at me.

A woman in a lab coat and glasses takes samples of the blood and places the broken window pieces into an evidence bag before labeling it.

"We need to keep an eye on this area in case it comes back," Robyn adds.

"I know they roam around down here, but usually they go for garbage cans, not people." I'm still shaking as they remove the body and place it on a stretcher.

"It's that time of year. They're getting ready to hibernate," Robyn says thoughtfully. "They can get crazy, but it's unusual for them to attack someone. Especially in this manner."

The EMTs carry the stretcher over the rocks to the ambulance parked on the bridge.

"Do you think the bear punched the window in to get to Bobby Dean?" I try to see the scenario in my head, and it doesn't seem logical.

"Around here, I've seen some pretty strange things. It might not be probable, but it is *possible*. I'll look into other angles of course, but don't come down here alone again for now."

"You don't have to worry about that," I tell her. "By the way, Augusta told me yesterday he got into it with a guy in the previous town over comic books. Doubtful that has anything to do with this, but I thought you should know."

She lifts a brow. "Comics?"

To those who are not collectors, it's difficult to understand that people might be obsessed enough to fight over books in general. "Bobby Dean got into it with a lot of folks, from what I've seen through the years."

I offer her the gist of the story, and she assures me she'll confirm with Augusta and the police there, in case a report was filed.

"Can we look through the camper to see if he had my missing spell book?" I query.

"This is a crime scene, Belle. You stay here, I'll do that."

Since I've already been all over the crime scene, I sort of disregard her order. I follow her, and watch as she goes in, careful not to move anything unless she has to, and only then with gloved hands. She may believe it was a bear, but I can tell by the way she's hesitant to disturb anything, that she hasn't ruled out the attack being from another human.

As she carefully and systematically searches the belongings, I'm sure she's making mental notes. She exits, but I already know what she's going to say. "Sorry, but I don't see anything even remotely like your stolen article."

"What about a hidden compartment?"

"Been reading those mystery stories again?"

I grin. "You know me."

"I'll go through the vehicles more thoroughly once I have photos and video of everything. I'll let you know if it turns up."

A new possibility is bouncing around in the back of my mind. Even standing outside the camper, I can hear the books inside—Bobby Dean's personal collection. They're expressing relief that he's gone.

Even his own books didn't like him, and I'm sure once Robyn begins digging into his past, she'll come up with plenty of people who are equally relieved. But would any commit murder?

The vision of his face and the claw marks makes me shudder. Could the person who stole the book have just performed their first spell?

My phone rings and I say goodbye to Robyn. Jayne and I hustle away from the horrible scene, and I'm both relieved and nervous to see it's Leo.

When I answer, the first thing he asks is, "How are you doing?"

Just hearing his voice calms my nerves. "I'd like to

say fine, but I'm not. I just found one of our vendors down by the river, and he's...dead. It's horrible. Robyn thinks it was a bear attack, but I'm not so sure..."

"A bear...?"

I can hear his surprise and I explain everything as Jayne and I come to the paved path. "This is going to be a black mark on the book fair, and although I didn't care for Bobby Dean, I certainly didn't want him dead."

"I'm so sorry you were the one to discover the body. Don't worry about the fair. It's an ugly fact, but this sort of thing may actually bring *more* buyers." I hear him rustling around and I visualize him up on the hill, so removed from the rest of us. "I'm also sorry to tell you that since the book is missing, Raven, my contact at Chicks with Gifts, won't be coming to look at it. She's still interested, though, if we find it."

"We?"

"I will do everything in my power to assist you in recovering it."

My chest warms. Jayne and I trek the path through the woods, her nose raised as if on the lookout for the bear. "Thank you. I appreciate it."

"Do the police have any new leads? The dead man was one of the men on the list that you gave Robyn, correct?"

I wonder how he knows, but he seems to know a lot for someone who stays in his tiny world inside the mansion. "Yes, Bobby Dean tried to buy it from me yesterday. Robyn searched his camper, but so far, no luck."

"Could it be at his booth?"

"It could." Jayne and I enter the park, and I feel relief that we encountered no wild animals. "I'll go look."

"I'll be there shortly to help."

His offer surprises me. "I'm already here, and it won't take long," I assure him.

He sounds slightly defeated. "Okay, but be careful."

"Of what?"

There's a strained silence before he says, "Belle—I mean, Miss Sherwood—I can tell by your tone you don't believe for a minute it was a bear attack. At least not an unprovoked one. Someone broke into your shop last night to steal a book containing spells to control wild animals. I have one of them, too, and you and I both understand what kind of magick that is. If someone is out there using it—"

"I know, I know." Jayne and I stop at the edge of the vendor tents and I rub my temple. "I'm safe at the fair, and whoever used it went after someone that no one here liked. I don't know if he crossed the wrong person, or if something else is going on, but I'll be careful."

We disconnect and I head for Bobby Dean's booth.

Before I even get inside, Augusta hails me. "Is it true? Is he dead?"

News has traveled faster than I expected, and

multiple vendors join Augusta, all wanting the story. I give them the basic details, leaving out the more gruesome facts, and Augusta helps me sort through Bobby Dean's collection for sale.

We come up empty, and I ask her to keep an eye on the booth. "Until Robyn clears it, we can't do anything with his stuff."

Together, we reinforce the tent flaps, and I head to the library to grab paper and a marker so I can make signs to tell people the booth is closed. While I'm there, I overhear Molly discussing romance novels with one of the patrons.

Mrs. Delacruse is offering to donate a box of her favorites, and Molly will have none of it. "Bodice rippers have no place here," she tells Mrs. Delacruse. "Those are shameful and not healthy for our readers."

"That's censorship," Mrs. Delacruse argues. "There is a romance section in the library, and it could use some updating. I appreciate the classics, but you need to move into the modern world, Molly,"

I decide to stay out of that argument and consider talking to Molly privately later. I personally love romance novels, and I know many in town do as well.

At Bobby Dean's booth, I hang the 'closed' signs and notice the fair has doubled its patrons in the few moments I was gone. There are folks swarming all over, a line three deep at Augusta's. She gives me a quick wave and a thumbs-up.

Jayne and I weave our way through the crowds, avoiding several locals who try to stop me to get the scoop. I make excuses to leave, making it to the book-store several minutes later than intended. I wave at Ruby, running the sidewalk sale and surrounded by customers. She's wearing her red cape to keep warm, and it showcases her long dark hair and fair skin. Uncle Odin is assisting her, a knitted cap over his white hair. I wish I could tell them what happened, but there's no time or privacy.

Inside Beanstalk Books, I apologize to Daisy but she barely acknowledges me since she is swamped as well. She hasn't even had time to set up the outside table. Jumping straight in, I help her work through the flood of customers and again evade answering questions about Bobby Dean and the break-in as best I can.

An hour later, I have a splitting headache and we are finally able to breathe. She offers me some over-the-counter pain meds, but I use a rollerball of peppermint and lavender on my temples instead.

She wants the low-down about what happened at the shop and this morning at the river. Uncle Odin comes in to check on us, and I tell them everything.

Daisy is shocked. "The poor bears in this area are going to be in for it if people believe it was an attack. I've never heard of such a thing around here."

My uncle shakes his head. "Say, I haven't had time to research that odd language," he says to me. "I will as soon as I can."

He looks tired and I send him home to lie down.

By three, I'm exhausted as well, and so is Daisy. A constant stream of customers has kept us hopping.

Her grandson, Martin arrives, a young college student who fills in when he can, and we insist she go relax.

Things slow in the late afternoon and I rig up the table while Martin handles the register and restocking shelves.

Zelle is running the sidewalk sale for Enchanted now. She's already heard the news. Both of us are a hit with passers-by, so we don't get to chat much.

Cinder refills the inventory as fast as Zelle sells out. Over the next couple of hours each of my sisters check on me, but I tell them I'm fine, even though I'm not, since we don't have privacy.

At one point, Ruby brings me a stool from our shop so I can sit down. She also gives me a cup of tea, for which I am grateful, and Jayne gets a bowl of water and some kibble.

At five, I help Martin close up. I move the table inside, and Daisy returns, feeling better after her nap and delighted at the amount of money we've made. We're out of flyers again, too.

She's excited about Saturday's event, and I'm happy for her. This could boost the bookstore considerably and stave off her financial worries.

When I say goodbye and leave, I find Leo standing at the Enchanted table, talking to Cinder. He seems pleased when he sees me, and I feel a renewed sense of energy. "I'd like to purchase a bottle of beard oil," he says.

Cinder catches my eye and winks at me. "I was just

telling Mr. Kingsley you're the expert on the male line of bath and body products."

At some point during the afternoon, the display window glass has been replaced. I wonder if Cinder used her carpentry skills or her magick to make it happen that quickly. Probably a combination since the place was so busy.

I motion for Leo to follow me inside. "I know just the thing for you."

The shop is warm from the late afternoon sun, and several customers mill about. When Leo and I enter, we receive bold looks.

Both Zelle and Ruby are assisting them, compelling their attention away from us. Matilda is restocking shelves. I try to shake off what happened last night and this morning and enjoy the success that Beanstalk Books and Enchanted are having. This time of year, we normally see an increase in sales, but the yearly book fair definitely brings more people to town. Some see it as an entire weekend of shopping, reading, and fun.

We've set up a small section at the rear of the store to hold the male line we've been testing all year. Sales have grown online as well.

"Close your eyes," I tell Leo. This is a trick Cinder always does with customers who don't know what they want specifically. Whether you're purchasing a candle, soap, or a body lotion, scent is one of the most important things to consider. "Let's see what you're naturally drawn to."

He looks at me warily and then does as I ask. "I'm sure whatever you suggest will be adequate."

Adequate? "No one should settle for *adequate*."

For beard oil, we have three scents. The first I choose is the Frosted Juniper. As I wave it under his nose, I'm delighted to see his facial reaction.

"That smells good."

The next is a lemongrass-mint combo we call GoodFellow. He seems to like this one, too, but doesn't show as much reaction.

The third is a musk and bourbon mix. "Mmm." He smiles. "That makes me think of long winter nights in front of the fireplace."

Yep, that's the one. "You can open your eyes now."

When he does, his expression is lighter, softer. The fierceness that clouds his eyes and keeps his jaw taut is gone. "So which is it?"

I hand him the brown bottle with the picture of a fireplace on it. "Long Winter Night."

He chuckles. "That's the name?"

I grin. "Sure is."

"You know your products."

I know people. And books. I snag one of our coordinating soaps from the shelf. "Use this on your beard daily. It will clean it and keep the hair from drying out. The oil will add softness and control."

He strokes his thick beard with one hand. "I do need help with that."

We both laugh, and I wonder if that's the first time he has in my presence. Like his voice, the sound is deep and low and feels like a blanket wrapping around me. "Try it for a week and let me know what you think."

He glances at the shelf and points at the Frosted Juniper line. "Why don't you give me some of that scent as well? That's the one that smells like trees, right?"

"Yes, it's one of my favorites. We also use the scent in candles."

"I'd like one of those then, too."

"Okay." I walk to our Enchanted Forest line and select one for him. "Is there anything else I can help you with?"

"Every time I burn this, I'll think of you." He takes it from my hands, his fingers brushing mine. "If you deem that there's anything else I need, please say so."

The sentiment strikes me right in the heart. I think about the candle burning on his fireplace and wonder what the magickal candlesticks will do. I'd like to ask him about that room—the rose, the clock, all of it. He's obviously no stranger to magick, and I wonder how much Finn has told him regarding Cinder and the rest of us when it comes to ours.

Before I can respond, he gives me that quirk of his lips that masks a smile. "You've had an exhausting and trying day. I should go. Thank you."

I don't want him to. As I ring him up, I try to find a way to let him know how much I appreciate him coming by, but I can't find the words. I wish one of my books were nearby to tell me what to say. Maybe poetry, or one of my favorite romances. I'm rarely at a loss for words, but suddenly, I can't find the ones I need.

As I hand him the bag, I see that ghost of a smile again. "If you need anything, please do call me."

Watching his broad back as he leaves, I sigh. Savannah, in a shaft of light from the window, meows at him as he passes by.

I'm still standing behind the register lost in my thoughts when Cinder and Uncle Odin bring in the table and sandwich board. Ruby cashes out her last customer and I help bag the products. Matilda, a sly smile on her face, finishes restocking and we close.

As soon as the door is locked and Cinder has flipped the sign, all of them turn to me.

"What?" I ask.

Zelle grabs my hand and leads me to the stairs. "You have some talking to do, sister."

"I'll make dinner," Ruby announces, on our heels.

Cinder, Uncle Odin, and Matilda bring up the rear.

Jayne and Savannah rush past our feet as Matilda claps her hands. Sparks of magick appear above our heads and cascade around us like miniature fireworks. "And the first thing we want to hear about is Leo," she teases.

The next afternoon, I decide to talk to Graham Geyer while the volunteers are packing up the last of the library sale tables for the day. The fair is going strong, books coming and going with a speed that almost matches the gossip flying around about the break-in at Enchanted and the death of Bobby Dean.

Robyn is stalled on both, no clues or evidence surfacing yet to link them or provide clear cut answers. She's still hopeful, but I have doubts either is going to be resolved quickly. Worse, I fear there could be more incidents.

Secretly, I've decide to investigate on my own. Mr. Geyer's run-in with Bobby Dean keeps sticking in my mind and I've decided to ask him some questions.

Cinder needs me to go to the bank to pick up cash for the register and Jayne and I are exiting when I run into Leo leaving the salon Zelle works at. All I can do is stop and stare.

His hair is freshly washed and trimmed. It appears my sister's taken several inches off. It lays in beautiful waves all over his head, soft and inviting to my fingers. His beard is also trimmed close to the jawline and I like it, although I realize it reveals a faded scar running from his ear nearly to his mouth. I never noticed it before, and it's barely visible, even as he greets me on the sidewalk in the bright sunlight.

"Fancy seeing you here," I say.

For the first time ever, I see his face light up with a real smile. Not forced, but an actual cheek to cheek one. He looks down, as if suddenly shy. "Your sister offered to clean me up yesterday." He glances up from under his thick brows. "Those were her exact words, in fact. Apparently, I have neglected my grooming of late."

Zell's tactlessness doesn't surprise me. "That's my twin for you. She tells it like it is, much like our godmother. If you ask for either's opinion, and you don't really want the truth, you better be prepared."

"Noted. Where are you off to? The bookstore? The candle shop?"

We begin walking, Jayne by my side. She lifts her head and marches in front of us, as if she's leading the pack. "Actually, I was going to talk to Mr. Geyer. He's a library volunteer, and he and Bobby Dean—the man who was attacked—got into it over a book. I don't know why, but I keep thinking about that and wondering…"

"If this fellow could commit murder?"

"Shh." I glance around, relieved no one seems to have overheard him. "Mr. Geyer would never do that. I simply want to find out if he went back for the book, and I have this…gut feeling I'll find another clue."

"Are you psychic, Miss Sherwood?"

I love the way the sunlight bounces off his hair. He's smiling again. "No, but I keep having this niggling sensation in the back of my mind. I need to talk to him."

We turn the corner to head downtown. The volunteers are packing up and Mr. Geyer is finishing with a visitor at the table next to the front entrance. He has his cat with him.

Shadows fall across his table, and the tabby, lying on the concrete steps soaking up a fading ray of sunshine, perks up when she sees Jayne.

The customer leaves with a heavy bag, nodding to us as she passes. Jayne greets the cat with a tail wag.

"Was it a good day for sales?" I ask when he greets us.

His wrinkled face breaks into a smile and he nods enthusiastically, shaking hands with Leo. "I'm heading to the storage shed to see if there are more boxes we can pull out for tomorrow. We've got nearly enough funds to buy that set of train books."

Mr. Geyer's grandfather worked for the railroad in the early nineteen hundreds and passed the love of trains onto his grandson. He's been drooling over a set of encyclopedias describing all of the different types throughout history and coveting it for the children's section.

"That's good news. I'm glad the library is benefitting from the fair as well as the vendors."

Mr. Geyer grabs a plastic tote to begin placing the leftover books in for the night. The cat jumps on the table and I stroke her head. She purrs, leaning into my hand and staring at Jayne.

Jayne ignores her play for my attention by sniffing a bush nearby. "I wondered if I could ask about what happened between you and Bobby Dean the other day," I say to Mr. Geyer, helping him stack copies into the tub. "The John Steinbeck novel, remember?"

His face falls and he rearranges the stacks. "That man was a challenging human being to get along with. It was a clean copy and I should have just paid the money."

"He *was* hard to get along with."

Mr. Geyer huffs. "Has anyone seen the bear that attacked him?"

"Not yet. According to my cousin, the local conservation group has been scouring the area for it, but they've come up empty-handed."

Mr. Geyer snaps the lid on. He scoops up his cat and scratches under her chin. "I'm sorry about what happened, even if he was mean enough to make a preacher cuss. Do you know what they're going to do with his collection?"

"Robyn sent me a text this morning that she's trying to track down his closest relative. So far no luck. I'm going to pack up his tent and open the space to someone else. It's late in the event, but maybe another local crafter will want to sell their wares."

"I'd be happy to help," Leo tells me.

Mr. Geyer stares toward the park. "You know Ronald got into it with Bobby Dean, too."

"Molly's husband?"

A nod. The cat rubs her head under his chin.

"Over a book?" Leo queries.

Mr. Geyer puts his cat on top of the bin and shifts both to the ground. "He wasn't trying to buy anything. He was attempting to sell a set of Reader's Digest books. I don't know why he took them to Bobby Dean, but maybe he tried others and no one wanted them."

Jayne sits near my feet. "I take it Bobby Dean didn't either?"

He begins breaking down the folding table. Leo steps in to help. "Thanks, young man," he says to Leo, then to me, "Ronald was all red in the face when he came back, and he still had the books in hand. He was quite angry, but wouldn't say what happened."

I ask a few more questions, but he doesn't know anything beyond that. Frustrated, I'm disappointed my hunch didn't work out. I guess I'd best leave intuitive hits to my godmother.

Or help myself to some of her potion.

CHAPTER

TEN

"Did that answer your question?" Leo asks as we stroll away.

"It points me to Ronald. I guess I should talk to him, too."

He seems to think this over. "Another hunch?"

Probably a dead end. "Both had a disagreement with Bobby Dean shortly before he was killed. I'm exploring all leads, and if any pan out, I'll share what I've learned with Robyn. It might help."

"Would this person have an interest in a spell book, or be pushed to commit murder over something as trivial as a collection of valueless publications?"

"There are people who love those old Reader's Digest editions, you know."

We pass a couple with two young children, and they give Leo a wide berth. "Regardless, they're not collectible and usually end up at thrift stores or in the trash."

My heart pings. Every book deserves a home. I make a mental note to suggest Ronald donate them to the crafters at the fair who can turn the unwanted volumes into artsy decor. "Neither he nor Mr. Geyer knew about my book, though, and no, I don't believe Ronald would harm anyone, but I must be thorough with my…"

I falter, afraid to admit my only detective skills come from reading mystery novels and bits of trivia I've picked up from Robyn.

"Investigation?" His voice is slightly teasing.

"Yes," I confess. *Good thing I'm writing a romance and not a mystery,* I think to myself. *I'm terrible at this stuff.*

"I know you're in high demand and quite busy, but could I buy you a coffee? We can brainstorm your ideas."

A flash of giddiness sparks inside my chest. "You want to hear my ideas?"

He stops and looks down at me. "Is that not agreeable?"

I can't keep the stupid grin off my face and I feel my cheeks heat. "I would love to, actually. The Perking Pot is two blocks over."

"Perfect."

Before I know what's happening, he takes my hand and rests it in the crook of his arm. We walk on.

Dogs aren't allowed in the shop, so we take a table outside, the setting sun sending peachy rays across the sidewalk.

Leo orders each of us a decaf, mine with the shop's famous pumpkin muffin creamer. I sit nervously smoothing my skirt and running my fingers through my hair. While I know this is simply coffee and conversation, a part of me hopes wildly it's something more.

A date.

I barely allow myself to consider the thought.

A few people, both indoors and sitting at another table, watch Leo as he returns. If they're locals, they probably know who he is and wonder about him being out and about.

His size is formidable, and even with Zelle's haircut and beard trim, I feel how uncomfortable he is under their stares. Although his appearance today is well groomed and softer than his reputation attests, he still draws attention.

As we settle in, the intense scrutiny makes me defensive. I flick a tiny bit of magick at the other customers that makes them mind their own business. Then I silently cast a protective bubble around us and Jayne.

The creamer adds the ideal amount of cinnamon and clove that tastes delicious. We sip in comfortable silence for several minutes as I try to sort through the ideas circling my brain. I want to jump right into discussing the bear attack and missing spell book, but decide to engage in less serious talk first. "I hate to impose on you again, but would you be interested in looking at a couple of antiques that I've scrounged out of our attic?"

He plays with his cup, his large frame completely engulfing the chair. "Are you looking to sell them?"

"If they're worth something. I don't know how old they are. In fact, there's one I'm not even sure *what* it is. Nonni said it's called a telephone table. She used to have one for their landline, but none of us know where this one came from."

"I'm happy to appraise them. If it's mid-nine-teenth century, I have a buyer who loves that sort of thing."

"Awesome. There are rooms in our place with plenty of furniture, I just haven't had time to get through it all. I assume, however, that old furniture is worth more than old books."

He sips his coffee and gives me a sad smile. "Unfortunately, that's true in most cases. What's your favorite novel?"

I smile. "Are you ready for this conversation?"

He chuckles. "You have more than one, I assume?"

"I could never pick one! I have dozens, maybe hundreds. We could start by fiction or nonfiction, then break it down by genres. Then by authors..."

He grins.

"I did warn you."

He takes a large sip, a few drops of his own undis-solved creamer lingering on his mustache. "I do as well, as you probably guessed from my extensive library."

Using a napkin, I lean forward and dab at his upper lip. He seems startled at the amiable, intimate gesture.

"You have something on your..." I motion at his upper lip.

"Oh." Embarrassed, he accepts my ministrations.

Heat rushes to my cheeks as his gaze is warm on my face. I take my time, wiping more than actually necessary.

A pregnant silence falls between us when I'm done and we both find great interest in our respective mugs.

"The fair is going well?"

"Yes," I rush to assure him. "Very well, outside of what happened to Bobby Dean."

More silence. Small talk is not always my strong suit and I wish I had a book in my hand.

"I don't mean to be forward," I finally state, "but there's something that's been bugging me that I need to tell you about."

He eases back, and I see wariness shutter his eyes. "What is that?"

"Did you hire Linda to be your curator?"

His pause is guarded. "I did. She has the experience, and stays out of my way. Why?"

"I don't like to speak ill about folks, but she was the librarian before Molly. She left under questionable circumstances, and word is, she was doing something unethical there. I don't know what, and I don't care. I doubt it was criminal in the strictest sense of the word, or the board of directors would have pressed charges."

He studies me for an uncomfortable moment. Jayne whines softly, sensing the strained air between us.

I refuse to fidget under his disconcerting gaze. "I just thought you should know."

He glances at a couple passing by, the woman flinching away. "I appreciate your concern, but it's unnecessary."

Why don't people see him the way I do? I reinforce our bubble. I finish my coffee and slip my foot out of my shoe to rub Jayne's belly. She's asleep in seconds. "So your turn. What's your favorite fiction novel?"

"Are you ready for this conversation?"

Disaster averted, I laugh. The awkward sound rings out and echoes under the awning. I flush slightly. "We should get together and compare notes," I announce. "Someday when we both have more time."

A smile warms his face, that tiny, reserved one I've learned to love. "I would like that."

Leo returns the empty dishes to the counter and we walk to Enchanted. It doesn't take more than a block before we pick up a cat follower, then two more.

I wonder what it is with Leo that attracts cats, and then I think about his name, his hair, his size. He's like an overgrown one himself, and I blush at the thought —I may have a dog as a familiar and constant companion, but I do love felines.

"Cats sure have a thing for you," I tease as a fourth joins the cluster behind us.

He glances over his shoulder. "They're okay."

"Do you have one?"

"No."

We're a couple blocks away, passing Molly's house. She's hung a flyer about the fair on her gate, and it makes me smile. She's not perfect, but she sure is a better person than Linda, in my humble opinion.

"Any pets at all?"

"None, I'm afraid."

I hook a thumb over my shoulder. "You might want to think about adopting. They're quite independent, like you, and pets provide lovely companionship."

Suddenly the cats screech in unison, lifting the hair on the back of my neck. I slap my hands over my ears, watching them dart off, terrified.

Molly's German Shepherd bursts from the side of the house, rushing the fence and barking madly at us.

"Poor kitties," I say, moving slightly back from the rampaging animal. "He scared them to death."

With a hand on my elbow, Leo guides me past as Jayne runs right to the fence, tail wagging.

"Jayne, get back," I command, but the dog stops barking and sniffs at her.

I chuckle. "She does have a way with other animals."

"She sure does," Leo agrees.

With no warning, the Shepherd raises its head,

peers across the street, and braces all four legs. I glance over, but see nothing.

Abruptly, he wheels and shoots to the house, tail between his legs. He bolts through the doggie door, leaving the flap swinging wildly.

Jayne faces the woods as well, head down. Her scruff bristles. A dangerous growl rumbles in her throat.

Leo drags me with him, backing us against the fence. The flyer crinkles beneath my back.

"What is it?" I ask under my breath. "Is it the bear?"

He shakes his head. "That's no bear."

From the shadows, three sets of eyes appear. They all have an odd blue tint.

My breath catches in my chest. My fingers tingle.

Heads lowered, the animals move slowly into view, stalking, preying.

Magick, dark and ugly drifts through the air.

Coyotes.

CHAPTER

ELEVEN

Leo steps in front of me, and Jayne stays by his side. "Pick up the dog," he says quietly.

I grab her and she wiggles in my arms, the growling continuing.

The leader lifts its nose and sniffs. The chilling blue eyes darken as he focuses on Leo. He's missing a notch in one of his ears. They flick back and forth like antenna, listening. His upper lip curls back, revealing sharp white teeth.

Leo takes another step toward them.

I grab for him. "What are you doing?"

The air fizzles with the dark magick, sending goosebumps cascading over my arms. An exchange of something happens between the two.

The coyote drops its head, makes a yipping sound. Another tense silence descends and none of us move. Then it wheels around and flees, disappearing into the shadowy woods.

The others do the same.

I'm shaking when Leo swivels back to me. He sees my fear and puts his hands on my shoulders. "It's okay, they're gone."

Jayne stops struggling and licks one of his hands.

"*Put me down*," she says telepathically.

She's my familiar but she's still a dog and driven by natural instincts. The last thing I need is for her to give into them and take off after the coyotes. I ignore her and ask Leo, "Did you see their eyes? What was wrong with them?"

He glances over his shoulder. "We should get you home."

He takes me by the elbow and sets a brisk pace. Jayne keeps a wary eye out, and I'm grateful Leo is with us.

"They don't travel in packs," he says. "Unless they're hunting big game."

Like humans? The thought makes me queasy. "Do you think...?"

"That whoever stole the book used another spell? That's exactly what I think."

Cold fear scuttles down my spine. "It's possible, isn't it?"

He doesn't answer. I hand Jayne to him. "Hold her. I need to call Robyn."

Awkwardly, he accepts the dog. She tries to lick his beard and face, and he rears back but she's persistent. If I weren't still frightened, I'd laugh.

My fingers tremble as I dial and report the incident. She's already left work but tells me she'll send someone.

Outside Enchanted, Cinder is wrapping up the sidewalk sale and getting ready to close the shop. Leo returns Jayne to me. "I'm going to see if I can track them. Stay inside."

"You'll do no such thing. It's dangerous. The police are on it. Come in."

"What happened?" Cinder asks. "Was someone else attacked?"

I hustle both her and Leo inside and lock the door. Ruby is behind the register and frowns when she sees me. "Are you okay? You look like you've seen a ghost."

"Try possessed coyotes." They're shocked when I explain what happened outside Molly's.

Cinder seems uncomfortable when I mention the spell book, shooting a look at Leo.

"He knows about magick," I tell her, "and he suspects as I do that it's possible whoever stole Grandma's book is now using it to control these wild animals."

Ruby makes a T sign with her hands. Her black hair swings with her dangling earrings. "Timeout. Everyone to the kitchen. This calls for tea."

As usual, she's right. A simple cup of steaming chamomile with lemon calms my nerves. I stop shaking but I can't keep a myriad of random thoughts from rattling out of my mouth, as we discuss all the things that have occurred in the past two days.

Leo is quiet through all of it, as is Cinder. Normally

when I'm stressed, I lock myself in my room and disappear into a book. This is no time for escapism, however. If someone is controlling animals, it's my responsibility.

Ruby sets a plate of misshapen candies in front of Leo and I. "Eat some chocolate. It will make you feel better."

I lift one and it's so soft, it folds over on itself. "What did you do to them?"

"My candy thermometer broke. They didn't set up like they should have. Still taste good, though." She winks. "Trust me."

Cinder sneaks one and nods as she chews—her stamp of approval. "You did the right thing calling Robyn. Nothing else we can do at this point. You've had a rough week." She pats my arm. "Sit here and relax. We'll fill the others in and see what they think."

She and Ruby leave. I'm suddenly ravenous and Leo and I devour the candy. The soft sticky stuff ends up all over our fingers, and Leo gets some in his beard.

I grab a paper towel, wet it, and attempt to clean it for him. He doesn't seemed surprised this time and the venture ends in lighthearted laughter. He returns the favor, using the towel to wipe sticky chocolate from my chin.

After all of the coffee and tea, I excuse myself to run to the bathroom. In the mirror over the sink, I see my cheeks are flushed, my eyes are bright. Even with the recent upsetting incidents, being with Leo makes me happy.

When I return, he inquires about the antiques, specifically the telephone table. I lead him to the workroom, currently under renovation, and to the corner where the furniture is corralled.

"This is a great specimen." He examines it and the tiny bench that goes with it. "I can offer you two hundred dollars."

My pulse leaps. "Sold."

While that's enough to buy my coveted book, it leaves nothing to add to the expansion fund. It's more important that I put the money toward that, but I show him two more pieces, and after examining them, he estimates they're worth a hundred dollars each.

Four hundred dollars. It's not much, but it's something. We shake on it, and he informs me Albert will pick them up the following day.

"I appreciate it. This is more than I had when I started."

His finger touches my cheek. "Yet you seem disappointed."

I keep thinking about my book. "Sorry, I don't mean to. You're very generous, and that will definitely aid our renovations."

I see the estimate Cinder has written on the chalkboard in the corner. Every time we clear extra profit, she subtracts it from the total.

We still need nearly three thousand dollars. I know we'll get there eventually, but it seems like months and months away before we have enough to finish her dream. Not to mention the fact I still haven't told her mine.

"There are many things I'd like to do if I just had more cash. I'm sure everybody feels that way, right?"

He tenses. The man standing in front of me is a millionaire! *Awkward*! It sounds as if I'm trying to squeeze a donation out of him.

I stutter, attempting to back track. "I didn't mean... I mean...gosh, that sounded wrong. It's just..."

He raises a hand like a stop sign, interrupting me. "Actually, I'd like to hear about your dreams and what you could do with more capital."

I shake my head. "Really, I shouldn't have said it like that. I appreciate you buying these things, and the beard care supplies yesterday. Your support is incredibly helpful."

He leans one of his big hands on the telephone table. The solidly built antique groans slightly. "It's a book, isn't it? Besides your remodeling. You need money to buy a rare edition."

He can read my mind. "There *is* a book I would like to buy, and selling the telephone table actually provides the amount I need. It's just that my sisters and I have a plan for this shop and any extra we make goes into that. I shouldn't take the antique money and buy a book with it, no matter how much I want it."

"Why is it so important to you? Is it one of your favorites?"

"It is, in fact. A children's book that reminds me of

my Mom. She used to read it to me all the time, telling me how love was magick. I imagined myself the heroine of the story." I sigh as the memories flood back. "I've been trying to track down a copy the past few years, and the Book Peddler—Augusta Pennyweather—found one for me. I figured it would be twenty-five, maybe fifty dollars. It's in *perfect* shape. Signed by the author even."

"That's great."

I'm dying a little inside just thinking about it going to someone else. "It truly is my dream book, but there's no way I'm going to spend two hundred on it right now."

"Hmm. That's a steep amount for a children's book. I understand the sentimental merit, though. Things associated with childhood can have great value to us and are often priceless when they remind us of our family."

"Exactly! It's not the copy itself, it's the memories associated with it that I most want to hold in physical form again."

"I'm sorry you can't purchase it right now. If you let me know the title, I'll keep an eye out for a cheaper addition for you."

I'm grateful he doesn't suggest buying it for me. Then I'd feel like I owed him. My heart is heavy, but I have hope again. "That's the best offer I've had all day, outside of coffee. I appreciate it."

We walk to the front of the shop. The light overhead glances off his newly trimmed beard and shows me that scar again. "I'd offer to give you a ride home in our shop van, but it's not running again."

"I've already texted Albert to pick me up."

"Does your family live around here?" I ask.

Instantly, his relaxed body goes rigid. I know I've said something wrong.

He absentmindedly rubs a finger across the scar. "My parents are dead."

"I'm so sorry. I know how that feels. Ours are gone, too."

From most folks this draws sympathy. Leo simply stares at the floor for a long moment, then pushes out the door, making the tiny bell overhead jingle. "Goodnight, Belle."

"Goodnight," I say, heart plummeting.

I lock the door and watch him climb into Albert's car, more curious than ever about him and his secrets.

CHAPTER

TWELVE

The county medical examiner rules Bobby Dean's cause of death a fatal bear attack.

Robyn informs me the next day he has no family outside of a sister in Detroit. She's insisted Robyn donate the books from his collection to the library. She claims to have no use for them, and from what Robyn relates, thought her brother was an aimless, troublesome man who should have found a "real" job, rather than peddling used books around the South. She went so far as to suggest he provoked the bear in question and "got what was coming to him."

Robyn, Augusta, and I pack up the books in the tent, and several officers deliver those from the camper as instructed. Molly deems we can sell most at the volunteer book tables, but as she's sorting through them, she creates a stack with a frown on her face. "No, no, definitely not," I overhear her mumbling.

The pile grows bigger.

I stop my sorting. "What's wrong with those?"

She doesn't even glance up. "We'll be throwing them away."

Over my dead body. "I've never put a book in the trash in my life and I don't intend to start." I walk over to look through them. "We have plenty of patrons who would enjoy these. The rest can be sold. Why would we junk them?"

I know why, but I'm not backing down today. After everything that's happened, my nerves are on edge and I'm tired of side-stepping her weird hang-ups about certain genres.

Her hands cease dividing them up and she fixes me with a glare. "The last time I checked, *I* am the librarian here, not you, Belle."

"That's true, but you're not throwing any away while I'm around." I grab the stack and march out.

Daisy waves when I push through the door, arms hurting from the weight. Jayne, who's in the window, jumps down and greets me, tail wagging, as I nearly dump them on the floor. A few still manage to fall, scaring the dog and causing her to jump back.

"What in the world?" Daisy bends to pick those up. Jayne edges forward to sniff at one.

I set them on the author's signing table that's ready for tomorrow, huffing out an irritated sigh. "Molly was going to throw these away. I couldn't let her do it. She wouldn't even entertain the idea of putting them out. I know there are folks in town who would love them, so I'm going to put them on ours."

Daisy clucks and shakes her head. "That Molly. She's got some funny ideas about what people should and shouldn't read. I'm beginning to think she's not the best person to be running our library."

"Unfortunately, I'm starting to think the same."

We sort the various hardbacks and paperbacks by genre, and a few are nearly brand new, so Daisy catalogues them to put on the shelves.

I set up and arrange the rest out there, grabbing one of the flyers to make a quick sign on the blank side to state that they're two dollars apiece. I tape it to an oversized Alice in Wonderland edition with beautiful illustrations. I wedge that between the stacks and feel just a bit self-righteous as three women descend on them and start snatching up copies.

"Tilly, here's a book on North American birds," one exclaims.

Her friend grabs it from her fingers and rifles through the pages. "Yes! This is it...a lapwing. That's what I saw this morning."

"Aren't they usually found near water?" her companion asks.

She lowers the book. "I'm telling you, that was the bird on my fence this morning. The neighbor's cat was in the tree near its nest and it was trying to draw the silly thing away."

My memory sparks with something I just read. "They're known for diverting the enemy from a nest of eggs," I tell them. "It's the wrong time of year for her to be protecting that, but one of my grandmothers noted in her journal she had a lapwing in her yard this time of year. A few must hang around, even though the biggest body of water is a hundred miles away."

The lady gently smacks her friend on the arm with the guidebook. "See? It's possible!"

I tell them I'll be happy to ring them up inside when they're ready and they barely acknowledge me, so enthralled with their new finds.

Back inside, I grab a box of mysteries and begin organizing them. I've purchased a dozen of each in the series and start arranging them in order, beginning with the first.

Daisy is humming and I'm thinking how sad it is that even Bobby Dean's sister seemed to find him difficult to get along with when Albert steps out from behind one of the bookshelves.

"Hello, Miss Sherwood."

I jump, dropping my handful. "Eep!" My hand flies to my heart. "You startled me."

He holds up both hands, one holding a novel. "Sorry. I didn't mean to."

The copy in his hand is the latest in the Benning's series. "I didn't realize there was anyone here besides me and Daisy."

"And your dog, of course." He gives me a perfunctory smile and helps me pick up the books I've dropped. "I'm procuring this for Mr. Kingsley. He plans to have it signed at the event."

"How nice. I didn't realize he liked mysteries."

"Doesn't everyone?" He scans the back cover,

reading the description. "Though, I believe he's purchasing it for a client who is unable to attend the signing."

"Isn't that Linda's job?"

Albert raises a brow and the bell over the door rings as Leo enters. "Hello, Belle."

"Leo. What are you doing here?"

He motions at the sidewalk table where the three women are still combing through the items. "I'll take all of them."

Daisy, emerging from the back, glances at me, then smiles at Leo. "I'll ring you up," she says happily. She winks at him. "But you may have to fight those gals for some."

Albert shows Leo the mystery novel. "Looks like I got the last one."

I point at the box at my feet. "I have more in here."

He smiles and places the edition on the counter. "Add this to the total for those outside."

"We'll grab them," I tell Daisy, and Leo follows me out. The trio take one look at him and decide they're done shopping, taking their armloads to Daisy.

"Why are you buying all these?" I ask him.

He doesn't look at me, taking several of the heavier ones from my arms. "I have a buyer who wants them."

This is a lie. "Is that so?"

His gaze flicks to mine, then away. "I'm sorry about last night. I realize I may have been gruff at the end of our conversation."

I'm just glad he's here. Once more, I think about

Bobby Dean and his sister, my parents. "Talking about family can be painful. I'm sure you miss your parents as much as I do mine. I never meant to pry or open up old wounds."

He stares me full in the face, searching it with his intense eyes. "You are a wonder."

Feeling heat rise into my cheeks, I brush him off. "Not really. I'm just..."—I shrug—"me."

As Daisy rings him up and I bag the books, Robyn arrives. She looks surprised but pleased when she sees Leo. "I'm glad you're both here," she says to us.

Albert grabs the bag handles. "I'll take care of these, sir."

Leo nods and addresses Robyn. "Did you capture the coyotes?"

The three women move to the counter to put their coveted finds on it, all giving us questioning looks.

"That odd pack caused havoc last night over at Graham Geyer's place," Robyn says.

"What?" I move around the register, leaving Daisy to ring them up, then I lead Robyn and Leo into the stacks at the rear, away from their prying eyes and ears. "Is he okay?"

"They went after his wife's chickens," Robyn tells us. "He chased them off, but later they showed up at the convenience store while Lonnie was closing up."

"The convenience store?" Leo echoes.

I can see them chasing chickens but why go there? Fear laces through my veins. "What did they do?"

Robyn withdraws her blue notepad from her

pocket and checks her scribbled entries. "They stood out front and bared their teeth at the men inside—Ronald Fitzgerald was buying milk and paying for gas. Apparently, one of the coyotes started ramming its head against the glass door. That's when Lonnie called us. When we arrived, they scattered. We couldn't pick up their trail."

Leo and I exchange a worried look. "These aren't your ordinary coyotes," he tells her.

"I'm aware. Both Geyer and Fitzgerald mentioned the weird blue eyes like the two of you witnessed. Could have been a trick of the parking lot lights. I've got the local conservation folks and wild animal organizations, and a hot shot from upstate who's an expert on them, all looking into it. On top of the bear attack, it doesn't look good. When you saw the coyotes at the Fitzgerald home, are you sure they didn't act rabid?"

"Aggressive, yes," Leo says. "But not rabid."

"I wonder if Ronald was home when the coyotes confronted us," I muse aloud.

Leo and Robyn both stare at me. "Why would coyotes be after him?" Robyn's sudden intense focus on me makes me want to clam up.

She's the expert on solving mysteries, not me.

Leo lowers his voice. "Are you having one of your hunches?"

More scrutiny from Robyn. "What kind of hunch?"

Embarrassment heats the back of my neck. "Nothing solid. Just throwing out ideas."

She watches me. "If you know anything, please tell me."

Should I mention the spell book? The magick I felt in the air around the brick? The coyotes?

I sense her bracing herself, expecting me to do exactly that—bring magick into the conversation.

"I need evidence," she says.

That sounds like a warning—magick isn't proof. I hold my tongue.

After an uncomfortable silence, she puts the notepad away. "Let me know if you think of anything else or have any more of those...*ideas*, Belle."

After she leaves, I release a tight breath. I walk Leo to the door. The women are gone. Albert enters to carry another set of bags out to a sleek, black vehicle parked at the curb.

"You're holding something back, aren't you?" Leo asks.

Jayne, in her spot in the window, wags at me. *"Tell him,"* she says.

"I'm spitballing, that's all. She can't prove that whoever stole it is using the incantations on animals, and there's no point throwing that at her. Like she said, she needs tangible proof. I don't have it."

"Yet," he adds and I find him giving me that crooked smile.

Out on the sidewalk, we stop to watch the butler loading the backseat. "That book you were coveting," Leo says, "have you reconsidered buying it? You only get a chance like this once in a great while. The expansion is going to take time, but the shop will always be there."

"That's true, but..." I feel guilty for being so torn. "My family is everything." I glance at Enchanted and catch Zelle's eye. She's waving two different bars of soap under a customer's nose, using the same technique I did with Leo and the beard oil. "That book offers a special connection to my mom, but the real one is here." I point to my heart. "It would be selfish to spend money on it instead of putting it into our fund."

He traces a finger over the back of my hand, still pointing at my chest. The touch sends warm sensations rippling over my skin. "Just think about it, Belle."

I have. Augusta asked me earlier if I'd made a decision. My guilt compounds as I think about it. I told her I hadn't.

But I *have*, it's just harder to follow through and give her permission to sell it to the other buyer. I don't want to let it go, the idea of not bringing that precious story home causes my eyes to tear.

Yet, as I watch Leo leave, I know it's what I have to do.

"Go on home," Daisy tells me when I reenter. "I'll close up."

I thank her and gather Jayne, stepping outside. But instead of heading to Enchanted, I go to find Augusta.

It's not fair to keep her from selling the book, but when we arrive at her booth to tell her I can't buy it, I discover the tent flaps down.

The crafter who moved into Bobby Dean's space

hails me. "You looking for Augusta? She went to the hotel early."

"Shoot. I guess I'll have to catch her tomorrow. "

The woman hands change to a gal buying a stack of old books wrapped with Christmas ribbon and secured with imitation holly on top. "Said she felt sick. Probably coming down with a stomach virus or something."

Defeated, Jayne and I stroll back to Enchanted. My sisters have everything under control and I feel the urge to spend a few moments in the turret room, surrounded by my great-grandmother's books.

As Jayne finds a comfy spot on the floor, I pull out a journal and start reading.

CHAPTER

THIRTEEN

Rain threatens the next morning, and we keep the sidewalk tables inside, both at Enchanted and Beanstalk Books.

I never made my gratitude offering to the weather gods, and the clouds gathering over town portend we may have a doozy of a storm later. When I tell Ruby I fear it's my fault, she dismisses my worries, ordering me to stay out of the woods, regardless.

"Did you know Eunice's best friend started the bookstore?" I ask my sister. "It was more maps and nonfiction then, but still. Pretty cool, huh?"

"Wow. That is a cool connection. It's like you're predestined to work both here and there."

Predestined. I hear Eunice's journal, sitting on the stool behind the register, speaking in my ear. *"Buy the bookstore."*

If only.

Martin is once again helping next door, freeing me

to do my rounds at the bank and check on the sellers before putting in my normal hours at Enchanted. The vendors are worried, but I have a backup plan for bad weather.

Our volunteer fire department expanded several years ago, and the previous building is now used for community events when needed. The large open truck bays work great and it has a small adjacent parking lot.

I call Robyn for an update on the coyote situation, and she tells me there's nothing new to report. Then I call my friend at the city council. "With the rain threatening, I need permission for the fair to move into the old fire station." It's something we've done in the past.

"You got it," she says. "I'll give the keys to Mr. Geyer and have him open things up."

I alert the vendors, some hastily packing and heading over, others weighing the odds of doing all that work for nothing. I check the weather app on my phone and see it claims only clouds and no rain. I attempt to reassure them, noting Augusta is still MIA.

Returning to Enchanted, I help my sisters pour soap for a large order for Mrs. Starling, then I run the register. The clouds dampen people's desire to go out and sales are slow.

Taking our overflowing trash can to the dumpster, I feel the heavy air. Thunder booms in the distance. Despite the prediction, it's going to rain. I ditch the can inside, tell Ruby I'll be right back, and dash to the fair to see if anyone needs help.

As I draw near, I glimpse Molly on the edge of the library parking lot. She's staring into the trees near the walking trail and I follow her gaze.

Fear shivers through me. I'm glad I left Jayne at the shop.

A coyote stands in the shadows of a white poplar watching her. The leaves whisper in the wind, a warning. His dark fur, paws, and black nose are nearly one with the gloom, it's only his eyes—that unnatural, eerie, light blue—that catch my attention.

The two are locked in some kind of strained, invisible communication. Either that, or Molly is so frightened, she's stiff as a board.

Ignoring the first fat drops of rain that hit my face, I run towards her, shouting her name.

The librarian startles, dropping her cane. She whirls to look at me. The coyote snarls once, flashing his canines as though I've spoiled his fun, and lopes off.

"Are you okay?" I pick up Molly's cane and hand it to her. "What are you doing out here?"

She takes it with a shaking hand. "I'm fine."

I walk her inside the library, the wind whipping strands of my hair across my eyes. Several volunteers are inside the foyer, having set up the sale tables there. One is Mrs. Geyer. They each say hello as I hustle Molly past.

"I don't know what came over me," she murmurs as we take the steps up to her office.

"You definitely shouldn't be out there alone." Below us, Mrs. Geyer is relating the tale about the rogue pack going after her chickens. I hold Molly's elbow as we ascend the steps. She's still shaking.

I get her to her chair, then call Robyn. "One of the coyotes was near the trail behind the library parking lot."

"Just now?"

"Yes. It has to be from the pack—it had those freaky blue eyes."

"I'll send animal control and a couple of my officers to search the area."

I thank her and make Molly a cup of tea. She acts as though she's in a daze, and I wonder if I'm going to have to run the place today. To my relief, Mrs. Geyer comes upstairs to find us. "Is everything okay? Molly, you're white as a sheet."

Molly sets down the cup, then grabs her cane and rises. "Fit as a fiddle. No worrying about me."

"If you could stay and help with things this afternoon, I'd appreciate it," I tell her. "I'd like to check on the vendors."

"No problem," Mrs. Geyer says.

"I heard about those awful coyotes coming after your chickens last night."

She makes a face. "Thank goodness they didn't get any!"

"Did the animals look...off to you?"

"What do you mean?"

There's no casual way to say it and not sound crazy, but I try. "Did you notice anything weird about their eyes?"

She and Molly exit for the circulation desk. "I didn't get a good look at their faces. Graham made me stay inside while he chased them off."

I discover Albert downstairs inspecting the sales tables in the foyer. One of the younger female volunteers, Betty, is laughing at something he said.

He offers her a charming smile. "I swear on my mother's Bible that's how it happened."

She laughs again and waves a hand at him. "I can't believe you're stuck in that big mansion all day, every day, with that boss of yours."

Her tone makes me defensive, as if she's suggesting Leo is some kind of monster.

"Mr. Franks," I interrupt. "What are you doing here?"

He looks over, surprised. "It's my day off." He shows me the two books in his hand. "Thought I'd grab some light reading."

That whole big library Leo has, and he has to come here to find something?

"We appreciate your patronage," I say, but I wonder if he isn't just getting out of the mansion. Leo claimed Albert used his library and he buys him books all the time.

Molly appears at the head of the stairs and begins

navigating her way down with her cane. She has a raincoat on and her purse over her shoulder.

"Are you going somewhere?" I ask.

"I need to run home for a few minutes. I'll be back."

She doesn't look at us as she rushes for the door. Albert's gaze follows her. "Hello, Molly."

At the door, she hesitates, but doesn't turn or respond. Then she shoves outside and is gone.

"You know her?" I ask Albert.

"Sure. We grew up together a few towns over. Our older brothers used to play ball at the sandlot, and we spent a lot of time down by the river." He gets a somewhat dreamy expression on his face. "Those summers are some of my favorite memories."

Through the window, I see Robyn and her officers arriving. I excuse myself to catch up with her.

Augusta is loading books onto a cart Mr. Geyer brought her, and she waves at me.

The wind whips past us, pressing our clothes to our skin. In the distance, thunder echoes, and raindrops smack my face and hands. "I take it no one else reported seeing that coyote?"

She shakes her head. "Nothing. The bear either."

She and the other officers start toward the trail. "Be careful," I call after them.

At Augusta's booth I help her, and Mr. Geyer offers us a second one. She accepts it. "How are you feeling today?" I inquire.

"Quite a bit better. Guess it was just a touch of

stomach flu." She glances up at the darkening sky, black and blue clouds roiling above us. "Good thing we're moving to shelter."

I agree and each of us takes a cart to push across the street. People are flooding back and forth, many locals joining in to help, making me proud of my community.

"I'm sorry to tell you, but there's no way I can buy the book."

She doesn't need any explanation—she knows exactly what I'm talking about. "You're sure? I can hang onto it for another day or so."

Lightning flashes and we both jump, hustling the carts into one of the large open truck doors at the old station. "It's all for the best. One of these days I'll have the money and I'll be able to find a copy to add to my collection."

I bring two more loads over, and head back to Enchanted. Just as I'm arriving, Leo meets me on the sidewalk. "I heard about the coyote. Is Molly okay? Are you?"

The rain finally cuts loose and we rush inside. I lead him past a few customers, nod at Ruby and Cinder, who are working, and take Leo into the back.

Grabbing several towels to dry with, I explain what I saw and how Molly was acting. "Ronald was at the convenience store last night. When we saw the pack, it was across from their house. There's a link between the coyotes and Fitzgeralds, but what? How?"

He rubs his hair, turning into spikes all over his

head. "Is there any connection to the bear and that Sutton fellow? Or it and the Fitzgeralds?"

"None that I know of."

His face is pensive. "I think we need to talk to Ronald and Molly."

"I don't think she feels good. She said she was running home for a bit and claimed she was fine, but she looked terrible. Maybe we can catch Ronald later when he comes to work at the book sale."

"What about the convenience store guy? Wouldn't hurt to get his firsthand report. We can compare notes on what we saw."

"Good idea." The storm is raging and I glance at the ceiling, the rain loud on the roof. Jayne hustles over to my feet. She's not a fan of thunder. "Should we wait a bit?"

Leo shoots me a crooked grin. "Will you melt?"

His teasing feels welcomed after the scary incident with Molly. I love staring at him with his hair wild, a wicked gleam in his eyes. For a moment, I simply soak him in, grinning back. "I may be sweet, but no, I won't."

He throws an arm around my shoulders, leading us to the exit. Jayne reluctantly follows. "Then let's go."

LIKE USUAL, Lonnie Vandru is behind the counter. Leo and I are thoroughly soaked by the time we get inside. On the way over in his car, I mentioned seeing Albert at the library sale. "I didn't know he grew up around this area."

"We both did."

That surprised me, and I realized again how little I know about him.

We shake off the rain and query Lonnie about what happened. Thankfully, the store is deserted, and he has time to talk. He doesn't seem to care Jayne is in my arms.

Tall and lanky, with acne scars and a slight lisp, he toys with a diet soda and watches Leo carefully as he relates the story. I have a feeling he's never seen Leo inside here before, but he knows who he is.

"Closing time, I was waiting on Ron, and he was taking his sweet old time getting some milk and bread. I had a date, and I was kind of in a hurry, but he was dilly dallying, making me a touch nuts, y'know?"

I nod in an effort to get him to finish.

"Them coyotes ran past the door and around Ronald's car out there near the gas tanks. At first, I didn't know what it was, I thought it was just some dogs. Then I saw them weird eyes they had." He flicks a stained finger toward his own. "I went to the door to look out at them. Ronald came over, too. Freaked no small amount 'cuz of Molly."

"Molly?" Leo and I say in unison.

Lonnie shifts his attention to me for a brief moment before it returns to Leo. "She was in the car. Didn't look all too happy about it, neither. She started honking the horn and flashing the lights. One of those dang coyotes ran right up to the door and was staring at me and Ronald, I flicked the lock, which sounds silly 'cuz no animal could open it, but I gotta tell you, it freaked me out. Them eyes…"

He shakes his head and glances at his soda can. "I never seen anything like that. That coyote meant to come inside."

His gaze bounces up to us, then down again. "It was snarling and snapping at us. We backed our bodies away from that door, let me tell you."

He tells us about the coyote ramming his head into the glass, two more circling the car and Molly. Jayne peers around my shoulder to stare out the door at the gas pumps.

Leo and I exchange a look. "None of the coyotes attacked her, right?" he asks.

Lonnie shakes his head. "Nah, she was okay. Police arrived, chased 'em off."

I glance at the parking lot, seeing the scene in my mind. "Did Ronald say or do anything else that you can remember?"

Lonnie fiddles with his soda, takes a big swig. "When it was over, all he did was pay for his groceries and leave. Didn't say a word, but when he got in that car, he and Molly squealed out of here like the hounds of hell were after them."

FOURTEEN

Now I'm suspicious of Molly. I decide to question her, but Leo insists we develop a plan first. Since I know she won't admit to anything involving magick, I have to agree.

I check on my sisters, but the storm is keeping people away, and they're handling it fine.

The vendors are okay as well. The library volunteers brought trays of sandwiches and ice chests full of soda and tea. Folks are chatting about books and enjoying the impromptu meal.

"I'm hungry, too," Leo claims as we're leaving the station. "Plus, I want to show you a book I have I think you'll like. How about lunch at my place?"

Jayne barks her agreement. My mind is whirling about Molly and the coyotes, but those thoughts disappear like fog on a sunny morning. Leo, his magnificent library, and a book he thinks I'll like...how can I say no?

On the drive to Millionaires Row, he mentions he's using the beard oil and likes it. We chat about normal things, rather than the chaos going on.

But as we're about to pass Molly and Ronald's, I grab his arm. "Stop. Plan or no, I need to question her before anyone else gets hurt."

Leo simply nods and pulls into the drive. "We should speak to her husband, too. Do you know what you're going to say?"

I search my memory for questions detectives ask in crime novels, but none seem right for this situation.

The maple in their front yard drips water on the sidewalk, and the flyer is laying soggy against the fence. Leaving Jayne in the car, Leo walks me to the door and rings the bell. We hear the dog bark inside.

When no one answers, I begin to think neither of them is home. "Molly must have gone back to work."

We're turning to leave when the dog falls silent and Ronald swings the door open. He glances at me, then Leo. "Yes?"

His face is blank, as though he doesn't recognize me. "Ronald, how are you doing after last night's incident?"

He shoots me an odd look. "What incident?"

"With the coyotes at the convenience store," Leo supplies.

As though Leo has startled him, Ronald glares at him. "What about it?"

"Are you okay?" I prompt.

He rubs a hand over his face. "Look, I'm not even sure they were coyotes. They were simply...big dogs."

Leo crosses his arms over his chest. "They weren't dogs. We saw them, across the street"—he points to the trees—"when we were walking past yesterday."

Ronald shrugs, stands defiant. "So?"

"Lonnie told us they had blue eyes," I reply. "Do you remember that?"

He sneaks a glance toward the woods. "Look, I already talked to your cousin. We've got a pack of wild dogs running around and they got aggressive last night. That's all."

I try to look past him into the house. "Is Molly here?"

"She's ill. I sent her upstairs to take a nap."

"A good idea," I tell him, even though I'm disappointed. "She doesn't have any new or unusual books lying around, does she?"

Leo gets my train of thought, but Ronald simply appears perplexed. "She's got books all over the place, but nothing unusual."

Questions exhausted; we're getting nowhere. Leo touches my arm and we say goodbye.

"The spell book has to be behind all of this," I tell him when we're in the car.

Leo taps a finger on the steering wheel. "We just have to find it."

CHAPTER

FIFTEEN

When we arrive at the mansion, the skies have cleared, and the sun is out. Jayne skips happily up the entrance.

Albert is off and Leo tells me Linda called in sick. It's just the two of us, and I'm looking forward to spending time with him, especially if it means being in that gorgeous space on the top floor.

He leads me to the kitchen, an enormous commercial stove and refrigerator in amongst beautiful wood cabinets and gleaming countertops. Ruby would be so jealous "My sister would love this kitchen," I tell him.

"I'm not a cook, but I can put together something edible."

"Anything will do. I'm starving."

We dig into the refrigerator and pantry, and a few minutes later, we have an assortment of cheese, crackers, and fruit.

"Be right back," he says. "I want to grab a bottle of wine from the cellar."

I feel nearly giddy. First coffee, now lunch. Is it possible Leo is as infatuated with me as I am with him?

The kitchen is so enormous, it has a spacious eat-in section overlooking an immense garden filled with fruit trees, wildflowers, and an assortment of god and goddess statues. As I'm admiring a beautiful wishing well in the center, movement catches my eye. Leaning forward to peer to the left, I see Albert and Linda on a brick patio, seated in elaborate wicker chairs. Linda laughs, the muffled sound grating on my nerves.

Guess we're not alone after all.

Leo returns and I mention that both are outside. "Linda must be feeling better."

"You're kidding." He looks slightly deflated, as he sets down the bottle with a *thunk* and frowns at the layout of food. "I mean, I'm glad she's well, it's just..."

I imagine he was going to take me out there for our lunch. "It's okay." I touch his hand lightly. "We can go upstairs."

He glances at me from under his bushy eyebrows. "You want to get your hands on my books."

I laugh. "Busted."

Jayne barks and Leo laughs, too.

The back door flies open, Linda's giggles echoing as she enters, the butler on her heels. They pull up sharply upon spotting us.

Albert seems surprised Leo's home. Linda blushes

and moves behind him as if embarrassed at being discovered. "We were about to head upstairs," I tell them. "Looks like you're feeling better," I say to Linda.

I can just see the top of her head over Albert's shoulder as it bobs. "Much. Just a bug, I guess."

"Seems to be a lot of that going around."

I carry the tray, and Leo brings the wine and glasses. As we pass the sitting room, I see the rose under the dome.

As if it senses my presence, it perks up. The full flower head turns toward me. Two more petals have fallen since I was here, their deep red color ringed almost black.

I stop to stare at it, and Leo looks back. "Belle?"

The clock murmurs, and like the last time, I see the candlesticks moving out of the corner of my eye. I hear books talking. Some about themselves; others are discussing Leo and me.

I try not to blush at what they say, moving toward Leo and the elevator. "Just admiring your decor."

After the doors close, we ascend to the top floor. Leo glances at me. "Sorry about that."

I shrug. "Seems your butler and curator have a secret romance going."

He makes a face, appearing horrified by that idea, and I have to laugh. I'm still concerned about Linda and her behavior, but if he's decided to keep her as an employee, it's none of my business. I hope this episode with her "illness" makes him look harder at her and her scruples. I don't believe for a minute she was actually sick, regardless of the fact there is something going around.

Emerging into the library is like walking into heaven for me. The smell of the books, the sight of their spines lined up on the shelves, and the openness of the room all welcome me in.

Sunlight streams through the large windows as we carry our lunch to the reading nook. Once there, we sip wine and make different combinations with the offerings. Leo serves Jayne on a tiny china plate and she gives me a glance to say she approves.

Once satiated, we savor another glass and review what's happened since I journeyed here to have him appraise my grandmother's books.

"There are no coincidences," he says, pensively. He lights the stacked logs in the fireplace and I eye the silver candelabra there, but it doesn't move. I tuck myself deeper into the comfy chair. "That book is tied to the animal attacks."

I agree, but the facts we know don't give us a clue about who is behind them.

When we've exhausted conversation about that, it turns to favorite books. Leo gives me a tour of his various collections, and I *ooh* and *ahh* over many. I could spend weeks in here, possibly months. Finally, he returns me to the chair and removes a wrapped gift from his desk.

He presents it to me and I smile as I tear off the paper. My heart leaps. I jump from the chair and squeal, throwing my arms around his neck.

Harriet and the Charmed Christmas. It's not *Harriet and the Magic Monster*, but it's the other edition in the series I don't yet have. I'm overcome with emotion. "How did you know?"

"I did some research. Also, I may have spoken to Zelle."

"You asked her what my favorite children's series was?"

"It came up during my appointment at the salon."

"Really? Doesn't seem like normal small talk."

"I happened to be captive in her chair at that moment and she regaled me with stories about you."

He grins, and I wonder what else he knows. I owe my twin, but I'm not sure if I should hug her or punch her.

As he takes it from my hand to set it on the table, our fingers touch, and we both freeze. Our eyes lock, and there I am, falling head over heels for him, amongst hundreds of books on the top floor of his mansion.

"This place is amazing," I whisper.

"*You're* amazing," he whispers back.

All around us, the book murmurs increase like radio static. Leo moves with a grace not seen in someone his size, coming close enough for me to see the brown flecks in his eyes.

His massive size dwarfs me, and his intense green gaze makes me feel as if I'll melt into the floor. "Belle, there's something I want to tell you."

I squeeze his hands, enjoying the feel of his long fingers and strong grip. "Yes?"

Just as he starts to speak, the elevator dings. The doors open and Jayne barks. "I brought tea and cookies," Albert's voice rings out.

Leo steps away and moves to his side of the table. "Ah, lovely. Thank you, Albert."

He motions for me to resume my seat, and the moment is over. Disappointed, I flop into the chair and scowl.

"Yeah, thanks a lot." Sarcasm drips from my voice.

The butler doesn't seem to notice. "Linda went home, and since I was already here, I thought I'd bring up refreshments for you two."

The phone on Leo's desk rings and Albert makes for it. I read through the book, and Leo watches me closely.

"I truly appreciate this," I say.

He smiles.

"Sir, it's Mrs. Haversham calling about the antique desk. She's leaving the country tomorrow and would like to finalize payment and the arrangements."

"I'm sorry," Leo says. "This could take a while."

I feel as if I'm being dismissed. I wanted us to have time alone again so he could tell me whatever is on his mind. I glance at my watch and stand. Jayne comes to attention. "I should get back to the shop and check on Daisy anyway."

"Albert can run you home," he offers.

The man nods and motions me to the elevator.

The look on my face must be enough to make Leo change his mind. He grabs my hand as I start for the shiny metal door and tugs me back. "I'll handle this as quickly as possible if you stay."

My heart soars. "Are you sure?"

"Allow me a few minutes, okay?"

I agree and he switches the call to his Bluetooth and wanders through the stacks as he speaks to his buyer. Albert fusses around, pours tea. "It's so nice to have company. A rare event around here."

"I'm sorry we interrupted your time with Linda."

"Nothing to apologize for. We were just chatting."

Right. I study the butler more closely. "Do you have a sweet spot for her?"

He winks at me. "You've found me out. I have a secret crush on every librarian. Their big brains fascinate me."

He seems to have a way with women. All except Molly. "So you and Molly...?"

Resigned sadness replaces his light tone. "She broke my heart in high school. It was a long time ago." He sets the teapot down and clears away the tray with the remnants of the cheese and crackers. "I hear she's happy and I'm glad."

Outside, a sound erupts that raises the hair on the back of my neck. I jolt out of my chair and rush to the window, Jayne following. "Did you hear that?"

He looks at me as if my head has spun around three times. "What?"

Behind us, Leo says goodbye to his caller. I scan the landscape below. "It sounded like... a howl."

With a shake of his head, Albert hurries to the elevator and punches the down button. "Sorry, I didn't hear anything. I'll leave you to the tea and cookies."

As Leo walks toward me, he holds out his hands. "What is it?"

I glance out the window once more but see nothing. "I think I'm imagining things."

I place my hands in his and allow him to draw me back to the chair. "You've been through a lot the last few days."

He's right. My world has been turned upside down. "Do you know much about coyotes?"

He sits forward in his chair. "You saw one of them?"

"I think I heard it howl."

He storms to the window and also scans the area. "They can travel over many miles in a relatively short time. I haven't seen any here in the hills. You're sure that's what it was?"

"No, but..." Jayne settles back in her spot near the fireplace, offering no confirmation.

Leo returns. "You're safe in here."

Nerves strung taught, I try to relax. I'm ready to talk about something else, and now's my chance to learn more about him. "Where did you grow up?" I ask, forcing myself to sound cheerful.

"In Wharton, a few miles away. I was a privileged,

spoiled young man. At least, until my parents died in a car accident shortly after we moved here."

"That's horrible. My parents were killed in one as well." The coincidence unnerves me, especially since Leo just insisted there are none.

"It was a hit and run. The other driver was never found."

"How awful."

He takes his chair and stares at the fire. "They had a fairytale romance, and I always thought I would as well, one day."

My pulse quickens and silence hangs between us. "My parents..."

"What?" He cajoles.

"They did, too. I believe it can happen."

We stare at each other for a heavy moment.

"Their deaths left me very angry with the world," he continues softly. "I didn't know how to take care of myself. Albert came along and took over, supporting me and keeping me from drowning in grief, but my inner rage wouldn't abate. I went on rampages in here, breaking things and creating havoc. Albert had the patience of a saint. Most of the time, he helped me keep that raging beast inside, pacified, but on the anniversary of their deaths every year, I would momentarily go crazy."

I set down my teacup. "That's completely under-standable."

"At times I became so depressed I wanted to die. During a particularly bad incident, I threw a large book at a mirror. The mirror shattered and a shard cut my face, leaving this scar." He touches his jaw line. "From that point on, I had no interest in my books or my money. I let my hair grow and the beard go wild. I wore nothing but old tattered clothes."

My heart goes out to him. "I also had dark times after mine were killed. There are still moments when I miss them so much…"

He leaves his chair as I choke back tears. He kneels beside me, taking my hands. "If there was anything I could do to take that pain away, I would."

I take a slow, deep breath, holding off the stem of my grief. I didn't mean to make this moment about me. "Along the line, you must have turned yourself around."

His hands are warm around mine. My much tinier ones disappear inside his. "One night I dreamed my mother came to me, and she told me it wasn't too late. That there was someone who would love me no matter what I look like on the outside and that that woman was coming."

His eyes are burning with a fire that makes me heat from head to toe. Behind it, I see fear at what he's admitting and I smile my encouragement. "Go on."

"She told me to stop drowning in my misery and live again. That my true love would soothe the rage inside and understand me like no one else could."

"What a beautiful dream," I murmur.

"I tried, Belle. I truly did, but it seems I'm cursed by my own hand. As the years have gone by, I've held onto that, but I seem to have grown more frightening, my features becoming more extreme. The way people look at me—it makes that rage come roaring back. My anger has a life of its own at times. That's why I lock myself away in here, searching for an answer."

Time has tricked me, or perhaps the clouds are back, because the room darkens as if the sun has already began its descent in the west. The candelabra on the mantle seems to light itself. Soft music plays in the background, and I realize it's the books. They're humming.

Serenading us.

Magick is afoot and my fingers tingle. This mansion is enchanted. Leo is as well. Not the dark magick that left a trace on the brick or is being used on the wild animals.

But this begs a serious question. "Was your mother a witch?"

He flinches and I kick myself.

"Leo, this house is infused with magick, and you are, too."

"I believe it's my mother's ghost haunting me." He says it with a sad smile. "The rose under the dome downstairs belonged to her, a gift from my father. It's been losing a petal each year on their anniversary, and I don't know how to make it stop. When the last falls..." He swallows hard. "Do you think her ghost will disappear forever?"

I wish I could ease his pain, but I don't know how. "The people we love never truly leave us."

He stands and paces to the window. "In the dream, she warned me to stop wallowing in my grief and seek out love. My time is growing short. The day after the dream, the first petal fell from the rose, and I realized she was right. That's when I let go of some of that rage, because I don't know how much time I have before my heart is frozen forever, love passing me by."

I join him at the window. "You're worthy of love."

"I'm cursed, Belle. I know it." He waves his hand toward the shelves. "I've spent every minute I can trying to find a way to break it, and I still haven't figured it out."

He turns to me, taking my hands and bringing them to his chest. "My search has led me to you. I believe you're the one who is going to save me."

My heart swells. I hear the books confirming that we are meant to be together. Jayne watches us, ears perked. The magick grows thicker, like a blanket wrapping around us. "Of course. I'll do what I can."

Hope lights his eyes. "I need justice for my parents. I've found evidence about the identity of the hit-and-run driver."

"We'll take it to Robyn. She'll help."

He dips his head toward mine and my eyes flutter shut. I tip my face up, ready for his kiss.

Before our lips touch, however, a woman's shrill scream echoes from outside.

CHAPTER
SIXTEEN

"Oh dear," I hear the teapot say.

"This can't be good," my cup answers.

"Of all the rotten timing," the candelabra growls.

I suddenly feel wild, untamed magick racing through the house. Dark, ugly magick.

The windows rattle, the shelves tremble. I command Jayne to stay as I hurry behind Leo down the actual stairs, bypassing the elevator.

Another scream rents the air from outside the huge mansion. It's as if speakers are inside my head, and the sound makes me slap my hands over my ears, gritting my teeth.

Hitting the first floor, Leo calls for Albert, but there's no answer. We hurry to the foyer and I hear a low growl coming from the Wild Beast book on the coffee table as we pass the sitting room. The rose is limp, the candlesticks and clock turn and watch as we zoom by.

Leo opens the great door and we run onto the veranda. In the drive, Linda is huddled near one of the urns, crying and pointing to the side. Her car is parked behind a clump of bushes under a giant tree along the driveway.

I see nothing unusual but my fingers tingle sharply and I can see the remnants of the dark magick floating on the air current.

Leo stalks forward slowly. I start to follow. "Be careful. There's dark magick at play."

"Get back inside," Leo orders.

"I'm a witch, I can help," I argue.

He swivels to face me, pointing at the house, but before he can issue another command, an animal jumps onto the roof of the car.

"Leo!" I point and he swivels to see it.

Bobcat. The animal's lips pull back into a snarl. The eyes glow ice blue.

Albert suddenly comes running from behind the house. "Linda, what is it?"

The bobcat leaps from the roof to the ground, swiping at him. It barely misses, long claws ripping through Albert's pants.

He cries out, grabbing at his leg and stumbling. Linda bolts toward him, her fear gone in the face of protecting him. She throws her arms out like a shield. "Stay away from my man!"

The cat stalks toward her and she freezes, sucking in an audible breath.

Leo grabs the butler, shoving him in the direction of the veranda, then jerks Linda from the cat. "Belle!" I shift my gaze to him. "Take Linda and get inside."

"I'm not leaving you," I argue.

The cat snarls. Leo plants his feet and expands his chest, making himself larger than life. "Enough!"

His command rings out and the animal flinches. I see the blue in its eyes fade, returning to a normal golden-brown. It backs up, shakes its head and lets out a growl that sounds more like Savannah than a wild animal. Then it rolls onto its back, and shows Leo its belly.

Overhead, clouds swirl, growing a purplish black, and I am both shocked and intrigued. On the porch, Albert hugs Linda and hustles her inside.

The cat was obviously possessed, like the coyotes, and the person who has the book of spells must be near. Yet, Leo somehow has removed the possession.

"How is that possible?" I murmur to myself. Magick is still sharp in the air, tingling the hairs on my arms as though lightening is about to strike.

Leo continues to stand over it, chest heaving.

"Whoever's doing this is close," I say softly to him.

The cat suddenly comes to its feet, hisses at me, and races off, disappearing behind the house. I fly to Leo's side. "Are you okay?"

His gaze follows the direction the bobcat went. "I'll have Albert take you home."

He's going to look for the book thief.

Without me.

"I'm not leaving. Whoever stole my book is using it to possess these poor creatures. Why do you think it was attacking Linda?"

"No clue. Look, this is too dangerous." Rain begins to fall, tiny bolts of lightning dancing over the house. "If nothing else, stay inside and help calm her down."

"I think it's Molly," I tell him. "She's controlling the animals."

He takes me by my arms and drags me onto the veranda to get us out of the rain. Then he gives me a tiny shake as if the action will make me come to my senses. "Belle, this is serious. These are vicious, wild animals. Whoever is doing this means business and is prepared to kill. Possibly already has. I can't let you seek out this person, be it Molly or not."

"Did you miss the part about me being a witch? I can handle her." The rain begins falling so hard, I have to raise my voice over the noise as it strikes the roof. "We're wasting time. Our thief is getting away."

He makes a soft growl in his throat. Anger flares in his eyes. Thunder booms and lightning flashes, illuminating the yard and drive.

Magick rides the wind. Suspicion blooms unwanted in my mind. "Leo? The possessed animals are afraid of you. They run off when you confront them, or do what that bobcat did and become docile." I search his face, praying I haven't uncovered a secret I don't want to know. "Why is that?"

"Just let me handle this," he says.

The cold burn of fear lights in my belly. I think back to our conversation when he said he was on the trail of whoever killed his parents.

He tries to pull me inside, and I yank from his grip. "You don't scare them." The realization makes me sick. "You have some kind of control over them, don't you?"

He shakes his head, rain flying from the ends of his hair. "You don't understand."

I stumble backward, grabbing the railing before I fall down the steps. "Then explain it to me," I yell over the noise of the storm. "Why are they attacking other people but not you?"

I see Molly and her limp. Think about her cane and the fact she became disabled from a car accident. Leo's parents, killed in a hit-and-run, the driver never found.

"It's Molly, isn't it?" My voice shakes. Could Leo have found a link to her and be seeking revenge? "You knew about the book. You know about magick and have been working with it, haven't you?"

That's why he has *Beasts and the Magick That Binds Them*. He's been trying to tame his own inner beast, but also attempting to find a way to bring justice to the person who killed his parents.

Not justice—revenge.

My grandmother's entry about the lapwing bird distracting the enemy to lead it away from its nest pops into my head again.

Leo wipes a hand over his face. "Come inside, Belle. Let me explain."

My heart shatters. All this time...all the distractions.

He takes a step toward me and holds out a hand. "Let's dry off and have some tea."

"You think I'd have tea with you right now?"

The door to the foyer is open, Linda and Albert gawking at us. Jayne saunters past them and comes to me. "Prove you're not the one behind the attacks," I challenge. "Come with me and help me hunt the real killer down."

His hand drops. His eyes go hard.

He leaves me standing there, stalking into the foyer and slamming the door behind him.

A sob breaks from my lips and I whirl to look down the long driveway. Instantly, the storm stops, the sun comes out. As I stand there debating my next move, birds begin to chirp and sing.

Jayne walks down the steps past me. *That went well.*

The sun is low on the horizon, sending swatches of peach and purple rays through the trees along the drive.

I need to talk to my sisters.

"*Yep,*" Jayne comments in my head. "*They'll know what to do.*"

I fly down the steps and we run.

When I reach Enchanted, Cinder is closing up. "What happened to you?" she asks.

I wave off the question. "I need to talk to all of you, now."

Five minutes later everyone is seated around the kitchen table and I'm pacing. Matilda crosses her legs and offers me a sip from her unicorn cup. Ruby suggests tea.

My twin chastises me. "I can't believe you ran all the way home with possessed animals on the loose."

"I hate to say it, but I believe Leo's controlling them."

Uncle Odin stiffens. "That's a serious accusation, my dear."

Savannah hops onto the counter and I'm so upset, I don't even bother to chase her off. "I don't want to believe he's doing this or is in any way connected, but there's something afoul about this magick, who's using it, and why. Maybe he didn't mean to take it this far, but I need to find out how Molly's involved, and maybe Ronald, too."

Uncle Odin adjusts his eye patch. "There was a time when we walked with grandfather bear and hunted with brother wolf. Those days are gone now, and we fear them."

Our uncle regularly talks like this, sometimes with no obvious point. But this time, Matilda pins me with her gaze and nods. "If you want to understand the beast you have to communicate with it."

I throw my hands up. "What beast? Or maybe I

should ask which? The bear? The coyotes? The bobcat?"

Uncle Odin smiles and raises his cup of decaf coffee. "No, my dear. The one inside your human friend."

Leo. "How exactly do I do that?"

Zelle rises from her chair and heads for the pantry. "Before you try anything with Leo and his inner beast, we should do a spell and uncover his true intentions."

As I glance around the table at my family, I see all of them nodding.

My heart stirs. Is it too much to hope I'm wrong? That Leo is indeed innocent?

SEVENTEEN

The spell is simple and straight forward and we gather at the table, me seated this time.

Clasping hands, we focus on the burning candle in the center. In radiating circles around it are layers of herbs, salt, and crystals. A few of Uncle Odin's runes are carved into the wax.

Savannah and the familiars are here now, too—Ruby's raven, Lenore, Cinder's hedgehog, McAlister, and Zelle's ferret, Rumpelstiltskin. Jayne jumps into my lap and stares at the flame.

Matilda has her eyes closed and I see them moving underneath the lids as she tunes into her psychic abilities. Uncle Oden stares at the runes and each glows a brilliant silver.

Cinder takes one of my hands, Ruby the other. Following suit, everyone clasps theirs together and Cinder nods at me to begin.

"I call on the unseen world to bring me clarity."

Magick snaps between us, a flow of white light running from palm to palm. My fingers prickle from it, as if I'm charged with electricity.

Once it completes the circuit, I direct it to merge with the candle. "I desire to know Leo Kingsley's true intention toward me. Let this wax, and this flame, reveal his face and his aim. May it be so."

"May it be so," the others echo.

The flame dances, higher and higher. It flickers side to side. Wax melts down the edge, touching a rune. My heart flutters in my chest like a trapped hummingbird, waiting...hoping.

The rune morphs into the outline of a face, murky and featureless at first. The silver glows brighter, Matilda tilts her head as if seeing the melting wax behind her closed lids.

Features begin to rise; eye sockets appear, then a nose. Ears and hair...

Not hair—a mane.

The nose elongates, a mouth appears. The ears point upwards on top of a broad head.

A lion.

Leo, the lion.

My breath hitches. This is the beast inside him roaring with rage. The wild feline predator the cats are so attracted to and the coyotes fear.

Matilda's lids snap open. She pins me with her eyes. Jayne also looks up from her spot in my lap. *"That's how he controls them,"* she says.

At the same time Matilda states it out loud, "King

of the jungle."

Leo's words from earlier ring in my ears... *That my true love would soothe the rage inside and understand me like no one else could.*

I have the ability to look past his outward appearance, even the fury inside him, and see the true essence of his being.

The flame gyrates and shimmers, revealing the outline of a flower. The petals dance and form a rose.

Big, lush, beautiful, the red shade is deep and vibrant. The scent infiltrates my nose and I breathe deeply, filling my lungs with that powerful fragrance.

"He loves you," Zelle says in a reverent, hushed tone. "He really does, sister."

Uncle Odin relaxes and gently slaps the table. "I knew I liked the old chap for a reason."

Cinder gives my hand a squeeze. "He isn't using the stolen book to possess animals and hurt anyone. His intention to help you find the culprit is true, as are his feelings for you."

I'm so relieved, a sob escapes my lips. Jayne nuzzles her head against my chest.

Ruby nudges me with her elbow. "Release the spell so you can call him."

"Thank you candle and flame," I offer, my pulse fluttering like mad. This time it's due to relief and the giddiness Leo brings. "I release you from this spell. So it is."

"So it is," the others repeat, and the flame returns to normal.

Our moods are much lighter as we clean up. I race to my room to phone the mansion, but no one answers. I bite my lower lip and stare out my window toward Millionaires Row. The night is dark and I can only make out a few lights in the far distance.

"Come on," I murmur, but it only rings and rings. No answering machine picks up and I finally disconnect, tossing my cell on the bed and then flopping spread eagle on it in frustration.

Zelle brings me dinner on a tray. I'm not hungry and ask her to set it on the desk.

She sinks down next to me on the bed, adjusting her braid that trails on the floor. "How does it feel?"

"Horrible." I sit up and hang my head. "I need to apologize and I can't reach him."

She teasingly pinches me. "No, I mean falling in love."

My emotions have ran the gamut from elation to misery. "It's a roller coaster! This isn't what I expected at all. I thought it would be like Mom and Dad's romance."

She places an arm around my shoulders. "Our parents had some rocky times, too. You just see the world through your rose-tinted glasses, Pollyanna."

The rose in the candle flame pops into my head. "I do love him, Zelle," I tell her, "and I will make this right."

"I know you will." She hugs me and leaves.

I'm more determined than ever to figure out who stole the book and is using the spells. Molly is still my number one suspect, so I reach out to Robyn. "There was an accident many years ago near Wharton, a hit and run, that killed two people." I give her the rest of the details that I know from what Leo said and ask if she can look into it.

She tells me she will. "Let's hope there are no animal sightings tonight."

After we disconnect, I call the mansion again. No answer.

"I should walk up there," I tell Jayne. "Demand he let me in."

In the window seat, we both stare toward the hill. "*Give him time,*" she suggests. She hops off and then onto the bed, snuggling into the downy coverlet and yawning. "*Emotions got the better of everyone earlier. Best to let things die down a bit. A good night of sleep and we'll all have a fresh start tomorrow.*"

Bent on resolving things between Leo and I tonight, I dial his landline once more. It clicks after the first ring and my heart skips. "Leo?"

But it isn't Leo, or even Albert. "He's not here," Linda grouses. "What do you want?"

A sharp retort is on my tongue, but I quell it. "Do you know when he'll be back?"

"No. He tore out of here like an incensed demon and we have no idea if he plans to return."

Behind her words, I hear the accusation—this is all my fault. "Can you give him a message when he does?"

"I'm not his secretary."

"Please, Linda. Just tell him I'm sorry and I need to

talk to him as soon as possible."

She hangs up, and I have no idea if she'll convey my message or not.

Worse, I don't know where Leo is.

Or if he'll come back.

"We have to look for him," I declare to Jayne, but she's already sleeping.

Matilda appears in my doorway. "Not tonight, Belle. It's too dangerous with these possessed animals running around, and you don't even have a starting place."

"I can do a protection spell on myself and we can scry for Leo."

She shakes her head. "Already tried. He's not showing on the map."

Frustrated, I collapse on the edge of the bed, disturbing Jayne. "Can't you...see him? Psychically?"

"He's cloaked."

"He's hidden himself from me?"

She leans against the doorjamb. "Or someone else is concealing him. He may not even know he's invisible to us."

I shiver at the thought. I hope with all my heart it's his mother's doing and not the guilty party behind the animal possessions. "He could be in danger."

"Pretty sure Leo can handle himself. Get some sleep, kiddo. I'll keep trying to locate him and let you know as soon as I do."

Heart heavy, I finally crawl into bed a few hours later.

CHAPTER

EIGHTEEN

I go through the motions of helping my sisters open Saturday morning, but my heart isn't in it. There's no word from Leo, and Matilda still can't find him.

I stuff the bank bag in my backpack and check on Daisy. The book fair ends at sundown and I know she's beside herself over the signing this afternoon.

She looks pale and tired when I arrive but assures me she's fine as she hands over the deposit. Martin is busy squeezing in a few more chairs for those who will be attending.

As Jayne and I leave on our errands, Daisy tells me to hurry back.

I hustle to the bank and then head to the park. Augusta is handing Linda a book and when I see which one, my stomach falls. "What is this?" I blurt out. "You're the buyer for *Harriet and the Magic Monster*?"

Linda barely glances at me. "It's for Leo's collection."

Augusta gives me a sad smile. "I'm afraid he was the one who wanted it."

Linda tucks it under an arm. "He has a client he does regular business with who's been searching for a signed copy for years."

A rough pit forms in my chest. "Is he back?" I ask.

"He is." Her tone is smug. "And he doesn't want to talk to you, Belle Sherwood."

As she stomps away, I fight the tears filling my eyes. Leo's home but won't speak to me. My beloved book is gone.

While I couldn't buy the novel and had resolved myself to finding another someday, it still stings to see it now out of my reach.

Leo's rebuttal does a hundred times more.

Augusta hands me a tissue. "I'm sorry, Belle. I really am. I'll keep looking. We'll find one."

All I can do is nod and walk away. Jayne heads for the library, and even when I try to call her back, she ignores me.

Fine. I'll question Molly.

But she's not there, and Mr. Geyer tells me she's feeling ill again.

When I return to the bookstore, Daisy is in the back bent over and holding her stomach. "I'm not feeling well," she finally admits.

I help her into a chair. She teeters as though she

might fall, so I hold her while calling an ambulance. "I think you've got whatever is going around." I tell her.

Martin darts in. "What's the matter, Grandma?"

She sweeps an arthritic hand through the air. "I have to be here for the book signing."

She's nearly in tears.

Her body sways to the side and we both steady her. I fear help won't arrive before she passes out. I order Martin to bring some water.

"Martin and I will handle the store. You need to lie down."

The ambulance arrives, and just as the paramedics are putting her on the stretcher, she does indeed fall unconscious.

I'm fearful about how quickly this happened and wondering what exactly this virus might be. The medics assure us she's simply dehydrated and will feel better in no time once they hook her up to an IV.

Two hours later, Martin and I are deluged with people filing in to buy books and get a good seat, even though the signing is several hours away. He's already checked on his grandmother and she is doing better, sending him back to the store for the signing.

Thank goodness, as customers are coming in droves, and at one point, I text Zelle, asking if she can lend a hand. It's nearly twenty minutes before she answers and informs me Enchanted is also swamped.

Paul and Tonya arrive to set up their table. I greet them and they seem pleased at the traffic in the store.

As Martin is ringing up a customer, I see his face

has gone pale and his eyes glassy. "Oh no," I say under my breath.

He suddenly dashes for the back.

I need to check on him, but I can't leave the register unattended, and Tonya asks me to get her a bottle of water.

"One minute, please," I say to her.

Hurriedly, I ring up the three patrons at the counter before dashing into the rear to check on Martin. The restroom door is shut and I hear unpleasant noises coming from behind it.

I knock. "Are you all right?"

There's a mumbling in the affirmative, but I know he's not. I grab a water and hurry to the front. As I hand it to Tonya, her husband, Paul, asks about the line out the door.

Glancing to the entrance, I'm shocked to see that people are still trying to file in and all the chairs are filled. Several folks have squeezed into the window, disturbing Jayne. I catch her eye over the shoulders of the audience and she winks at me, letting me know she's okay.

"Hello, everyone." I clap my hands to get the crowd's attention, and some of the noise dies down. I do it again, but half aren't listening and continue to talk.

A sudden whistle, sharp and piercing, rings out over the room. Thick, tawny red hair and broad shoulders push through the line. People scramble away from Leo as he walks toward me. "Cease," he bellows.

The crowd falls silent.

"Go ahead," he says to me in his normal voice.

I issue instructions to a few of the men to cram several displays between the bookshelves. Leo helps. It's not much, but it adds enough space that we're able to squeeze in another dozen.

Martin emerges, still pale and shaky, and I tell him to go upstairs to his grandma's apartment. He thanks me and leaves.

Leo touches my arm. "Is there anything else I can do?"

"I believe that's it." I scan his face, wanting to say so much more, but realizing we have a captive audience, the pregnant silence deepening as the crowd watches us.

Paul clears his throat and I tear my gaze from Leo's. "Yes, right. Welcome everyone!" I smile and motion to the authors. "Beanstalk Books is pleased to host Paul and Tonya Benning here to close the book fair and answer your questions about their award-winning mystery series!"

Thunderous applause. The couple stands and Paul gives a brief introduction, once the crowd settles. They read favorite passages and answer questions from the gathered fans.

Most ask about the main character, the beloved Ginger Madding, and the authors go on and on about her like she's a real person. The crowd eats it up.

Leo stands close to me, and as we laugh at a funny

scene with Ginger and her sidekick dog, Laramie, I see Jayne snorting along.

The laughter nearly drowns out the bell over the door as Albert and Linda—holding hands—squeeze in. Two people rise from their chairs, folding them up and creating more standing room.

The extra space still isn't enough when Molly and Ronald arrive, hovering on the threshold. Several more seated attendees get to their feet so the couple can press inside.

"Do you outline your books before you begin writing, or do you just sort of wing it?" Mrs. Derringer, who's sitting three rows back, asks Paul and Tonya.

They share a bemused smile. "I like to plot everything out," Paul answers.

"And I hate it," Tonya adds. "I like to go with the flow."

The group titters and another raises a hand. "How do you figure out who the bad guy is, and which clues are important, before you even start writing?"

"Everything is a clue; everyone is a suspect." Paul taps a finger on the book in front of him. "A good mystery needs plenty of red herrings."

This makes that niggling in my brain start again. *Everything is a clue; everyone is a suspect.*

Scanning the crowd, I glance at those connected to the stolen spell book, the animal attacks, and each other.

Molly, my main suspect, and her husband.

Leo, who I've eliminated.

Albert and Linda.

Even Augusta and Mr. Geyer are here, and I put them on my mental list, while my logical brain argues that neither could be involved.

Bobby Dean Sutton goes on it, too, regardless of the fact he's dead.

Then I mentally shuffle through the other elements: *The Beastly Book of Spells*, the book on Leo's coffee table, the broken window, the thief.

The fact nothing else was stolen from Enchanted, the truth that Bobby Dean annoyed everyone he met, Leo's parents killed by a hit and run driver, Molly's limp caused by a car accident.

The strange illness going around.

The magick in the mansion and the traces of dark magick floating around the brick and the wild animals.

I picture all of it laid out in front of me like a chess board. People and elements overlap, glittering threads running between them.

Someone asks another question and Tonya answers, drawing more chuckles from the crowd. Deep in my own mystery, I smile as if I'm paying attention

I imagine Paul and Tonya's character, Ginger, looking at each of the threads weaving in and around the main plot. In my mind's eye, I see her crossing things out, illuminating others.

I barely notice Albert slipping by, or sense Linda's disappointment at him leaving. I do notice Molly frowning at him as he passes her and Ronald. The bell over the door jingles, jarring me, and I feel the urge to follow the man.

But I can't leave, nor can I quite put my finger on why Ginger is telling me to look deeper into him and his connection to Leo.

Linda sidles up next to me and lowers her voice. "He has to get back to work. I should be going, too." She glances at Leo. "That book you wanted is on your desk."

I know which one she's talking about and my stomach flip flops. She begins making her way through the crowd.

Before she reaches the door, a woman screams. "Look!"

The sound echoes through the bookstore, and people scramble, although they're packed in like sardines. The books around me tense and Jayne begins barking frantically, throwing her solid little body against the glass in a frenzy.

"Coyotes!" Mrs. Derringer yells, and the crowd surges and jostles, some wanting to see, others struggling to get back.

Leo quickly maneuvers people out of the way so he and I can get to the door to see what's going on, but it's a fight. His broad back blocks my view, and I have to weave and bob to get a glimpse at what's outside.

Three of the animals line the sidewalk, peering in. Their bright blue eyes are somewhat vacant, but they growl and show their teeth at Jayne. The largest, with the notch missing from his left ear, approaches.

Pressing his wet muzzle to the glass, he snaps at Linda on the other side.

She gasps and spins around, shoving by Leo and nearly knocking me down in her effort to get away.

"Lock the door," I cry, and Molly reaches to grab the deadbolt.

Just as her fingers touch it, the coyote lunges, slamming into the door and knocking it open several feet. More screams and cries erupt, and the coyote hits the glass again to push his way in.

Leo jumps and bangs the door shut with a crash, throwing the deadbolt.

Paul and Tonya's table is knocked out of the way, stacks of mysteries tumbling, as people scramble over each other, heading for the back of the store.

I reach in my pocket for my cell but it's not there. "Everyone stay calm," I yell, forcing my way through the agitated crowd to the register. Another fight but my phone isn't there, either. "I'm going to call the police."

I squeeze past more folks to reach the back room and the landline. I hastily dial Robyn.

She doesn't answer, and I leave a voicemail, then call the main department desk.

The operator who picks up assures me she'll send several officers right over.

When I return to the register, Leo is standing guard at the door. The alpha coyote seems to have his gaze locked on Molly through the display window. His lips tremble and saliva drips from his mouth.

Jayne is still there, snarling and swiping at the glass like a miniature lion, but he pays her no attention, his gaze riveted on Molly.

If she's controlling these animals, why doesn't she send them away? Why is Notch Ear so intently focused on her?

I need some magick and fast. If only I had my phone to call my sisters, or had thought of doing it when I tried to contact Robyn.

Some detective I am. I push to the front and Leo.

He keeps his gaze riveted on the beasts as he murmurs to me, "Keep everyone inside. I'm going to chase them off."

"No!" I grab his arm, the thick muscles under my hand rock hard. "No one's going outside; the police are on their way."

As if Notch Ear hears my words, the coyotes howl in unison, throwing their muzzles skyward. The sound sends chills racing over my skin.

The echoes die off and the three size up Jayne through the window. Leo snatches her and hands her to me. "Keep the dog away from the glass."

Before I can stop him, he flips the lock, glares at a frightened Molly, and strides out.

CHAPTER

NINETEEN

Leo raises his arms and yells. I do the same time, but I'm inside and he's not.

The coyotes rush him, and by the time I hand Jayne to Mr. Geyer and reach the door, they're attacking.

Molly grabs my arm to stop me from running into the foray but I shove her off and she stumbles into Ronald. I grab her cane and launch myself outside, calling up all of my magick.

My ability is unlike my sisters. Cinder can literally step into people's shoes and know their thoughts. Ruby heals through food and touch. Zelle transforms others, allowing their true self to shine.

Me? I hear books talk and I play with words. Fighting possessed coyotes is well out of my wheelhouse, but I know how to weave a spell.

Speaking low, I throw a protective spell around myself. Poking one of the coyote's snapping at Leo's pant leg, I touch Leo's back, extending my magick to him.

The animal is shocked into immobility and Leo kicks him away. Notch Ear, already clamped on Leo's right arm, is flung off, landing on the sidewalk in a heap. The third plants all four paws and snarls, but keeps its distance.

Leo wheels around to face me, fierce anger in his features. He grinds his teeth. "I told you to stay inside."

"And I told you not to come out here," I counter, using the cane to point at the beasts. "These are no ordinary coyotes, and even if they were, you can't take on all of them by yourself!"

A snarl much like the coyotes' growls issues from deep in his throat. "That's where you're wrong."

The possessed creatures are up and begin circling us. I sense those inside watching and wondering. Fearing for us.

Leo grabs my shoulders and flips me around, putting his back to mine. "Don't take your eyes off them."

"We should be safe in the bubble."

"Bubble?"

"Of protection," I tell him. "It's magick."

The tinkling of the overhead bell filters to my ears, alerting me someone's opened the door. The circling coyote in front of me turns its gaze to the perpetrator, and before I can yell at them to close it, I hear Molly's voice cry out, "Get back in here!"

As one, the coyotes lunge. Leo shoves me aside and leaps in front of them, forming a barricade.

I stumble and fall, the cane dropping from my hand. My bubble of protection rips apart and my shoulder bangs into the brick wall. Pain lances my skin where my shirt tears and the rough surface draws blood.

The coyotes attack Leo once again. I cry out, fear getting the better of me.

All three attach to his body in various places, and suddenly a roar goes up like I've never heard. The hair on the back of my neck shoots up and gooseflesh races over my skin.

In front of my eyes, Leo morphs. His carefully groomed hair breaks free; his beard grows long in seconds. Muscles stretch, the seams of his clothes tearing.

His hands, fighting to grip the coyotes by the nape, lengthen. I scramble on my hands and backside, but trying to find the words to erect another protection bubble don't come. Leo has turned into something I can't understand, can't wrap my mind around.

When he spoke of the beast inside him, I never thought he was being literal.

Gaining my feet, I grab the cane and start swinging.

Molly has wisely slammed the door closed and several men are holding Linda back. I hear the click of the lock falling into place.

It's just me and Leo against these possessed creatures.

I wouldn't have it in me to hurt them under normal circumstances, but I have no choice if I'm going to help save Leo. Beast or not, he can't fight these three and their magickal controller on his own.

Between the two of us, we manage to gain the upper hand, and as I reach for Leo, the words once more flow off my tongue. "Magick protect us. Magick keep us. Magick bless us!"

I reach to touch Leo's back and he bats my hand away so hard I stagger. In the depths of his beast's rage, he doesn't know me from the animals attacking him.

My sisters emerge from Enchanted. Their eyes go wide upon seeing the scene. As several clients try to follow them, Ruby chases them back inside.

Leo throws the coyotes off but they return again and again. Zelle grabs me and the other two take positions outside the circle of Leo and the three possessed animals. Cinder and Ruby try to distract the coyotes, but fail.

Leo is bleeding from bite marks and gashes. I try to get behind him and work my way into the space between him and the bookstore, but every time I get close, a coyote gets in my way, or Leo's strong hands knock me back.

In the distance, sirens ring out, but my relief is short-lived. A savage bellow comes from across the street. Zelle and I glance over and see a black bear rising onto its hind feet and lumbering toward us.

"Take the bear," I yell at Cinder. She and Ruby throw up a wall of magick to keep it from gaining the sidewalk. Like the coyotes, its eyes are blue, unseeing, driven by an evil darkness possessing it. It claws and rages against the invisible wall and Cinder yells at me, "Hurry, Belle, whatever you're going to do, you need to do it now!"

Zelle jerks the cane from my hand, stomps in and wedges the end of it into one of the coyote's mouths. The animal stumbles, and I grip the coarse fur on the back of the second, the words of a spell I read in our grandmother's book flooding my mind. It's as if she's right there speaking them into my ear.

The coyote goes limp in my hands. Swamped with relief, I let it fall to the ground.

The leader of the pack is still attacking Leo, but now Leo has the advantage. He manages to loosen its jaws from his thigh, just as I step forward and slap my hand onto Leo's shoulder.

The coyote barks in pain as Leo's strength and my protective spell work together to disengage the beast's jaws. Leo tosses the animal several feet and it lands on its hind quarters, crying out again before the blue glow fades in its eyes.

The bear stops clawing at the magical wall and returns to all four feet. It shakes its head and lumbers across the street toward the woods as two police vehicles arrive. The coyotes manage to rise to their feet and run off as well, trailing past the bear into the park.

But the beast in Leo is still on a rampage. He looks for the next attacker and I see a pale blue tint in his eyes.

"Leo." I reach for him. "It's okay. They're gone."

The light grows brighter, and the next thing I know, one of his big hands knocks me in my injured shoulder and sends me to the ground.

I hit hard and suck in my breath. My gaze locks with his. He gives another hair-raising howl, and before I can say anything to calm him, runs away.

"Belle!" Zelle helps me to my feet.

The cruisers pull up to the curb. Molly unlocks the door and people stream out. The officers exit their vehicles and within seconds, I'm engulfed in mayhem. Even Jayne has to fight to get to me. Lifting her in my arms, I nuzzle her face, hearing people talking about Leo and telling the police he attacked me.

"No," I say, raising my voice to get their attention. "That's not true!"

Ronald ignores me. Zelle and Cinder try to lead me to Enchanted to examine my wound. I refuse, fighting my way to Ronald as he begins rallying people to chase after Leo.

"I'm okay. He didn't hurt me," I tell everyone, but it seems as though no one is listening. One of officers motions at Ronald to get in the squad car and they take off toward Millionaires Row.

"Wait!" I yell, but it's too late. "What are they

doing?" I cry to my sisters. Jayne wiggles from my arms. Matilda and Uncle Odin emerge onto the sidewalk.

Like the beasts who were controlled by magick, the people around me now seem to be possessed with anger. Their adrenaline is still high from what they witnessed and they're turning on Leo. A mob forms, folks dashing for the hill with arms raised and voices shouting for justice.

I can't stand it. Calling on all my power, I yell at the top of my lungs. "Stop!"

Many do, ceasing their frenzy and falling silent. But the mob headed to Leo's seems too far away to be affected. They are running.

I have to get there first. As Robyn pulls in and leaps out of her car, I tell Zelle to fill her in. I race past all of them and climb in.

"Hey," she shouts, but I throw it into gear and take off.

I speed past the angry mob and the other police car. When I get to the gated entrance, it's closed. I bail from the vehicle and climb the iron fence to throw myself over. My body aches all over from the fight, but I grit my teeth when I land on my rear and suck it up. I have to get to the house and find Leo before they arrive.

Trembling, I clamber up the porch steps and bang on the door. "Leo! It's me, let me in!"

It isn't Leo who opens the door.

"Miss Sherwood," Albert looks me over from head

to toe, his gaze lingering on my torn blouse and bleeding shoulder. "I'm so glad you're here. Perhaps you'll tell me what happened?" He motions me in. "He's upstairs. I haven't seen him this way in years."

"I'll explain everything after I talk to him." I scramble for an elegant staircase. I have no patience to wait for the elevator.

My foot falters on the step when I hear an odd click behind me.

"Actually, Belle, there's no need. This will be a tidy wrap up to my plans."

My mind flashes back over my mental chess board. In the chaos, I forgot who the most likely suspect might be.

Halting on the stairs, I turn.

A large, black gun is pointed right at me. His face above it, Albert smiles.

CHAPTER

TWENTY

Upstairs in the library, I find Leo injured. The beast has receded and he's back to his ordinary self, but he's barely conscious. Blood seeps into the expensive rug near the fireplace where he's fallen.

Jerking my arm from Albert's grip, I rush to him, falling on my knees beside his large body. The coyotes did a lot of damage and it's difficult to determine which wounds are the more serious, but one stands out—a hole on his upper left chest that leaks blood with every pump of his heart.

"You shot him?" I glare at Albert. "You despicable, no-good, selfish man!"

"Belle," Leo gasps.

"Shh." I tear off the jacket I'm wearing and press it into the puncture to slow the bleeding. "The police are on the way."

Behind me, the butler chuckles. "I have a strategy of keeping them out."

I hear his footsteps receding and I glance over my shoulder. At the desk, he flips through pages of a book. "Let's see...which spell should I use this time?"

The Beastly Book of Spells.

He recites one under his breath and outside I hear the scream of a vulture, the trill of raccoons, the raging roar of another bear.

Soothing Leo's brow, I ask between gritted teeth. "Why are you doing this?"

He moves to the front of the desk and leans against it, crossing his feet at the ankles. The gun is slack in his hand. "I tried using Leo's edition downstairs, but the curses didn't work quite right. Not strong enough. But yours..." He wiggles a finger at me. "Your grandmother was a real witch. She knew what she was doing when she wrote those incantations."

"My grandmother is not the author of that sorcery. She was a white witch, like me."

He shrugs. "Believe what you want. Makes no difference. Her book has real power to it. I tested the first on that Sutton guy. The bear was hard to manage, though."

Leo's eyes flutter closed. His hand reaches for mine and I clasp it. "Why in the world would you want to?"

"I've been trying to find something to control Leo for years, and now I finally have it."

"You're loathsome!"

"You and that big vocabulary of yours." He grins at

me. "I don't come across many like you, Belle Sherwood."

The compliment turns my stomach. Outside, I hear people at the gate. "I won't let you get away with this."

He laughs, a snide sound that crawls up my spine. "Unless you've got a black magick streak in you, you don't stand a chance against me."

A warlock. "I should have known. The magickal fingerprints on the brick and around Bobby Dean's body. It was your magick."

"What can I say?" He glances around at the room. "Luckily, this place has enough of Anna May Kingsley's magick to cover it up."

"She was a white witch, too, wasn't she?"

"For all the good it did."

"You're going to be okay," I tell Leo softly.

Closing my eyes, I think about the magick running through my veins. I imagine my sisters, my mother, all of the women descended from Eunice, and I call on the books in this house, the magick Leo's mother left behind, and try to channel all of it into Leo. Behind my eyelids, I see energy sparkling and flowing to him.

Perfect. Now to distract the perp. "Why would you do this to him?" I ask Albert. "I don't understand why you want to control him. He trusted you."

He walks over, a frown wrinkling his brow. Maybe he realizes I'm trying to heal Leo. "Originally, I just wanted to get Molly back."

"How does this help you? Unless I'm way off base,

scaring a woman to death is not usually the best romance technique.”

I hear shrieks from outside and flinch. Whatever animals he's called up to protect the place are dangerous.

“Molly isn't your average woman. I tried blackmailing her into coming back to me years ago by threatening to tell the police she was the one who killed Leo's parents. I even threatened to tell him myself.”

I knew it. “I take it she refused to play that game.”

He sits in the chair, watching me with a bemused expression. “She told me if I wanted her back, I wouldn't want her thrown in prison. Can you believe it?”

He's crazy. Psychotic. “So you thought possessed animals would woo her?”

He chuckles at the sarcasm in my voice. “I sent the coyotes after Ronald. I figured if I took him out of the picture, and showed her my power, she might rethink her feelings toward me.”

Leo's breathing is growing labored, His eyelids flutter open and I see the depth of his pain, both physical and emotional. “Belle...”

I shush him and murmur a healing spell Cinder often uses in the lotions. “How do you know Molly was the driver?”

He waggles the gun. “This is where it gets interesting. She swerved to miss a coyote—not a dog like she claims—that was standing in the middle of the road that night. One possessed by me. I'd been messing with Leo's book and discovered that lone animal was weak enough to control. The spell was feeble and the thing fought it. As I was forcing it to bend to my will, it ran into the middle of the road and just stood there. Molly was driving too fast, and when she spotted it, she jerked the wheel. The car slid and just so happened to ram into the Kingsleys coming from the other direction.."

Leo stirs. The bleeding has slowed to a trickle. The magick is working.

"Now, thanks to that book of yours, I can control Leo's beast. All I have to do is compel him to kill you, and then I'll shoot him in self-defense. Guess who inherits the mansion?" He points a finger at himself. "After all these years of taking care of him, I'll be free and rich! He's got no one else. I'll get Molly back, and together, we'll live a very good life."

Underneath my hands, Leo's chest rumbles. When I glance down, it's not the man staring at me through those green eyes.

It's the beast.

CHAPTER
TWENTY-ONE

Leo's animalistic rage is uncontrollable as it launches him off the floor, knocking me aside to go after Albert.

I tumble into a chair and it slides off the rug, both of us crashing into the hearth. The table that held our lunch, tea, and cookies the day before teeters and falls.

Albert hurriedly raises the gun, but Leo barrels into him before he can fire it.

His chair flips tailfeather over teakettle with the two of them.

Boom! The gun goes off.

Leo roars, the butler screams. The chandelier overhead is hit by the bullet, shattering the light. Crystals in the shape of teardrops rain down.

I throw my arms over my head, the men flailing and rolling about. Even though Leo is extremely injured, his rage is burning bright. He grips the other man's wrist and crushes it, forcing his hand open.

Albert cries out and the gun clatters to the floor. I scramble over and kick it away.

When I glance back, Leo is choking him.

I reach out to Leo but hesitate. What happened downtown is still fresh in my mind. I know how hard it is for him to rein in that part of him—if I'm not careful, he'll lash out at me.

"Leo Kingsley, you are not a beast!" I don't touch him, but I drop to my knees and try to catch his attention. His eyes are pinned on his butler. "You are *not* a murderer. You are not like Albert. Let him go. The police are here, they'll take care of him."

The beast flicks his glittering, angry gaze to me. He snarls, ferocious, but I don't move.

Once more, I stretch out my hand, not touching him, but imploring him all the same. "Come back to me, Leo. Let go of the anger. Let go of the rage. We know who killed your parents, and now you can get justice for them. You can also release Molly from her burden of guilt, because even though she fled the scene, it wasn't her fault it was standing there. This is Albert's doing, I understand how angry you must be at him but killing him isn't the answer. He needs to pay for what he's done, not get off the hook so easily."

Leo is breathing hard, his nose flaring. He glares down at Albert, who's turning blue from the pressure on his windpipe.

And then he eases up.

I keep my voice soothing, even though I'm shaking with fear and my own anger. "That's right, Leo, you're a good man. You deserve to be happy and loved. I'm here, and your mom was right. You are worthy of love, and I need you."

Albert's gagging, and I know he doesn't have much time left. My hand hovers in the air between me and Leo.

In the background, I once again hear the books murmuring. My grandmother's on the desk is speaking to me. I close my eyes and tune into it, listening to what she chants in my ear. My lips start to move, and the magick flows.

Not a spell. A blessing.

The Beastly Book of Spells may have belonged to her, but she never used it to control animals. I hear her voice telling me how she took it from someone misusing magick and planned to destroy it. She used her own white magick to find those animals being controlled by a wizard and reversed his curses, blessing the poor beasts and severing their connection to him.

May all beings be blessed.
May all beings be free.
May magick bring love to all.
May magick bring love to me.

As I continue, I fill my heart with love for Leo.

"It's working," I hear a candelabra say.

"Keep going," the wall clock adds.

A ripple goes through the house, white magick, pure and untainted brings more voices. "The rose!"

"She's saved us!"

"She loves him!"

Cheers go up. The magick inside flares brighter and I sense a presence—Leo's mother.

When I open my eyes, her ethereal spirit hovers near him. She reaches out a hand and passes it over his head. I see the beast in Leo fall away. He's once more a man...

The man I love.

His head shifts and his gaze locks on mine. He's bleeding again, but the wound is trying to close on its own.

With heavy movements, he slumps off Albert, limp on the floor, and I crawl to meet him halfway.

His strong arms embrace me and I melt into him. For long seconds, I listen to the beat of his heart and know I'm home.

Then he sets me back, hands holding me at arm's length as he examines my wounds. "Oh no. No, no, no," he mutters, voice strained. "Did I do this?"

"I'm okay, Leo."

His face contorts with dismay and he releases his grip as if afraid to touch me. "Belle, you have to get away from me."

Before I can argue, the elevator dings and the police, along with my sisters, rush in.

TWENTY-TWO

The fair closes the next day, the excitement of the previous week bundled up with tents and boxes.

The vendors begin pulling out of town by noon, and I'm sad to see them go. Luckily, Augusta decided to stay a few extra days to help at the bookstore. Daisy and Martin are feeling better, and Daisy is home, but at her age, recovering from a sudden illness takes time. She's decided to take a break to recoup, after insisting Martin return to his classes at the university.

Leo was treated and released from the hospital, his wounds healing as if by magick before the doctor got a look at him. According to Finn, the bullet wound completely disappeared prior to the ambulance getting him in the clinic door.

Robyn arrested Albert, and I gave my statement regarding his role in what happened. I also related the information he divulged about Molly.

Because she's not comfortable believing in magick, Robyn finds it hard to wrap her mind around the fact Albert used spells to possess wild animals, and that his ultimate goal was to control Leo's inner beast. I'm not sure exactly what she's going to put in her official report, and she still has *The Beastly Book of Spells* in her possession as evidence, but I don't think I want it back anyway.

She stops by Enchanted to inform us Molly turned herself in before she could be arrested. Leo refuses to bring charges against her, however, because of Albert's involvement. The butler, fearing Molly was going to be sent to prison, admitted to causing the accident.

Molly still left the scene of the crime, but Leo has procured a lawyer for her, and Robyn believes she'll get off with a lifetime of community service. Albert, on the other hand, is being brought to justice.

Gossip flies as the vendors pack up, and someone claims the library board fired Molly. A message on my phone from the president confirms this, her voicemail inquiring if I'd consider the position.

I return her call and encourage her to extend the offer to Mrs. Geyer.

Leo is shunning me. I've texted, called, and visited the mansion multiple times since the previous evening, but he won't respond. Matilda scries and confirms he's inside.

My cuts and bruises are healing, thanks to Ruby's magick. I was so wired I couldn't sleep, so I sat in the turret with my laptop and began re-writing the romance. It helped me process what happened, and another session tonight might finish the story.

Sunday dinner is always at Nonni and Poppi's farmhouse, and we have lots to tell them over her delicious chicken and dumplings.

Most of their questions are directed at me, but I have a heavy heart and find no joy in retelling the events. Uncle Odin keeps reaching over and squeezing my hand in support.

Snow and Runa have come, too, and brought a gallon of the farm's famous apple cider. After the main meal, we get a healthy sugar fix with a tray of Ruby's candies, and conversation turns to talk about the remodel efforts and her plans to turn her candy-making enterprise into a business. She explains she has a new friend a few towns over who runs a successful gourmet candy shop. The woman is also a witch and has quite an interesting background.

Nonni mentions how excited she is about the upcoming fall festival. Snow assures everyone the giant pumpkin will make the perfect Cinderella coach for Fairytale Land, the biggest tourist draw around these parts. She grows one every year for this exact purpose.

Cinder surprises me out of the blue with a question. "Finished writing that book yet, Belle?"

Matilda grins at my shocked face. "There wouldn't happen to be a handsome and charming hero like Leo in it, would there?"

Flustered, I don't know what to say. "How did you know?"

They all chuckle. Cinder winks. "There's not much you can keep from us, sister. You know that."

My twin, seated next to me, pinches my leg. "Give him a few days," she advises, more serious now. "Leo's devastated that he hurt you and he's giving you space."

"I know, but I don't want that. I want him."

Zelle gives me a knowing, sad smile, and the rest begin cleaning up.

Snow invites us to the orchard to pick a bushel after the dishes are done. Nonni goes with us, and Uncle Odin and Poppi stay to discuss other things.

At the farm, I greet Snow's miniature rescue animals, including Sweet Pea, her Baby Doll sheep. Her foreman is down with a bad back, and like us, she's extremely busy this time of year. She's been trying to find a replacement, but so far hasn't had much luck.

Returning to Enchanted in the late afternoon, we're loaded down with Macintosh, Jonathon, and a new variety Snow created by grafting several of her dwarf trees together. We're laughing, and I feel halfway normal, until I discover Linda waiting for me in the parking lot.

I rush to her hoping for news about Leo. "Is he okay?"

"He fired me," she grounds out, then rants for another minute. "He thinks I was helping Albert! Me! I had nothing to do with any of that..."—she makes a face—"witchy stuff. I had no idea what he was up to, you have to believe me. You have to talk to him. Tell him I'm innocent."

I do believe her, but it miffs me that she's more concerned with her job than Leo's state of mind. "He won't answer my calls or come to the door."

She rubs her temples and paces. "He was packing boxes when I was there. You don't think he's moving, do you? He said something about this town hating him. He said *you* hate him."

"What?" Now I'm livid. "I don't, and he knows it. If he wasn't so stubborn, I could tell him exactly how I feel!"

Linda rushes at me and grabs my hands, squeezing them hard. "You have to get through to him, Belle. Whatever it takes, talk some sense into him. He can't leave town! I need that job."

Jerking my hands out of hers, I set my jaw. "Do you ever think of anyone but yourself, Linda?"

She leaves in a huff and I go inside. My sisters ask if I'm okay and I lie and say I am. Cinder sets up the tools to make a batch of Halloween soaps in the shape of cats and questions if I want to help. I beg off, claiming I need time to finish my story.

Upstairs in my window seat, I stare toward the hill. Jayne climbs into my lap and licks my face. I pet her absentmindedly, and finally, she jumps down and disappears. When she returns, she has her leash between her teeth.

I accept it and scratch between her ears, loving the

soft feel of her fur. "You're right. We can't let him leave, and more importantly, we can't allow him to sit and stew, believing we hate him."

Together, we say goodbye to Cinder and head for Millionaires Row.

TWENTY-THREE

The curtains are drawn, the house lifeless. No one answers the door and it's locked.

Jayne and I hang out on the veranda for hours, and I attempt to communicate, regardless, telling Leo I refuse to leave until he opens the door and speaks to me.

There is no reply of any kind.

The sun goes down and the air chills. Defeated, I take Jayne home.

Laptop in hand, I ascend the hidden staircase to the turret to work on my book. As if my sisters know me well, which they do, Ruby has left a plate of candy, and Cinder, a black cat candle that smells like cloves and magick.

As I type away, the books on the shelves hum and chatter. Anytime I get stuck, I hear words flowing into my ears giving me ideas.

Monday morning dawns rainy and overcast. It's

the first of October and my day to run the shop. I put off the bank deposit and like most Monday mornings, things are a bit slow. I don't mind, enjoying the quiet time while Zelle and I inventory products and design new displays specifically for Samhain and Halloween.

Typically, I hum along to the overhead music and delight in a cup of tea as I restock shelves. Now, everything seems as dull and colorless as the clouds in the sky. Even the fragrances of the candles and soap bars fail to cheer me.

Zelle leaves for the hair salon for her first appointment, and Matilda takes over the register so I can run next door and check on Augusta.

She waves when she sees me. "Belle! I'm having so much fun!"

The store has a single customer, and she informs me she's spent most of the morning cleaning up from Saturday afternoon's event. She's also created a display of books on vintage items and antiques, and shows it off proudly. "Do you think Daisy will like it?"

Just seeing the books makes me think of Leo, and a hollowness burns in my chest. "She'll love it."

Back at the shop, I tackle taping fall festival flyers in the windows, and arranging the black cat soaps and candles my sisters made last night. As I'm working, Jayne gives a single bark from her bed in the front window. Savannah in the other seat hisses.

"That's weird," Matilda says, and I follow her gaze to the sidewalk. "Did Ruby bring home another stray from the forest?"

Cinder, Ruby, and Zelle are always finding home-less animals, some injured or starving, and fostering them until they're ready for a forever home.

On the other side of the glass door is a gray and white striped cat. It looks slightly familiar. "Huh," I say, looking closer. "I think that's one of the feral cats that was following Leo and I before Molly's dog scared them away."

"Doesn't appear feral now," she comments.

The cat wears a collar studded with rhinestones, and there's a tiny lavender colored envelope clipped to it like an ID tag. It sits patiently, staring through the pane at me. "I think it wants in."

As I approach, it raises its paw and scratches at the glass. I open the door and see my name is written on the envelope in bold handwriting.

"Thank you, kitty." I unclip it and the cat rubs against my ankles. Jayne barks, Savannah hisses, and the tabby meows once before shooting off.

Matilda walks over as I examine the envelope. "What is it?"

Peeling it open, I find an elaborate white and gold invitation inside. My gaze falls to the signature, but I already know who it's from. "Leo."

Matilda leans in. "What does it say?"

"He's inviting me to dinner." I glance at her, unable to keep the smile off my face. "Tonight."

Matilda gives me a playful jab. "Zelle was right. He just needed a day or two."

My head is in the clouds the rest of the day, and I

can hardly focus on customers. By the time we close, I'm as nervous to venture to the mansion as I was last week.

I gather a selection of soaps for him, and add a few of Ruby's candies to a bag. Zelle helps with my hair and makeup, and Matilda insists I wear a pretty velvet jacket over my corduroy skirt. With my sisters and godmother sending me off, Jayne and I head to his place.

When I ring the bell, the door swings open, but there's no one there. Magick tickles my skin, and I feel the presence of Leo's parents inviting me in.

"Hello?" I call.

There's no answer. I'm drawn to the sitting room where the rose twirls under the glass dome. The clock hums a cheerful, rhythmic tune. The candlesticks sway and dance, as the books beckon me to go upstairs.

I take the elevator to the third floor. My pulse skips as it rises and I try not to fidget.

When the doors open, I gasp at the beautiful sight before me.

An elegant antique table rests near the fireplace, candelabras burning bright and dozens of platters of food set on a golden tablecloth. The china and sterling silver gleam and catch the candlelight, and I hear the books chattering away, excitement in the air.

Leo stands at one end beside a stately looking chair with a high back. He gives a slight bow and pulls it out for me. "I'm glad you came." He motions for me to sit. "Please, come and dine with me."

The teapot clears her throat. A teacup next to her whispers. "Be our guest."

Leo clears his throat. "I mean, would you be my guest?"

I want to run to him and throw my arms around his neck, but instead I smile demurely as I venture over. "Thank you for inviting us. I brought you a little something."

I hand him the bag of soap and candies. He takes them, gratitude brightening his somber features as I sit.

"How are you feeling?" I ask as he fills our wine goblets and takes a seat at the opposite end of the table.

"I'm recovered. And you?"

The exchange is stiff and formal like the old Leo. My heart sinks, longing for our closeness and wondering if I can call it back. "Can we forget the small talk?" I ask and plunge on. "I miss you. My world isn't the same without you."

My outburst makes him uncomfortable. He folds and refolds his napkin before meeting my eyes. "I can't tell you how sorry I am about everything that happened."

Magick swirls and a platter of appetizers moves toward me, as though an invisible butler is serving us. I place several on my plate. "I'm fine. Really, I wasn't hurt."

Candlelight flickers across Leo's features. "It was my fault. I should have handled things differently."

"You protected me and saved me from Albert. You guarded the bookstore and all of those inside from the coyotes. You're a hero, Leo."

He coughs as if flabbergasted. Again, he attacks his napkin before he finally sets both hands on the table. "You are an amazing woman, Belle."

Heat rises in my cheeks.

"Is everyone okay?"

"Yes, fine. Well, Daisy's still recovering from her stomach illness, but that has nothing to do with you."

He makes a face. "It may, actually."

"What? How?"

"That kind of dark magick can affect nonmagickal individuals who are sensitive to it, causing physical illness."

"I didn't think of that." I sit back, disconcerted. "They all had contact with me. I was the common denominator."

"You can't blame yourself."

I tick the list off on my fingers. "The spell book, the brick, Bobby Dean, the coyotes...I was immune to the traces Albert's sorcery left behind, but I spread it around."

"You didn't know, and I'm sure Daisy will recover like the others have."

"I sure hope so. She's already so frail, and I don't want her to lose the bookstore. If only I could..."

"Could what?"

We've gotten off topic. "Nothing. It's a silly pipe dream."

"There's no such thing."

It's my turn to play with a napkin. The cotton is soft and pliable as I wring my fingers in it. "I want to buy the store and merge it with Enchanted."

His brows rise in appreciation. "Do you, now?"

"You must keep it a secret. I haven't even told anyone else, not even my sisters."

His fingers make a zipping motion across his lips. "It's a wonderful dream."

I sip the wine and stare into the fire. "One that won't happen, but so be it." Setting the glass down, I lean toward him. "The people in this town don't hate you, Leo, and neither do I. I don't know why you would think such a thing, but it's time they learned how special you are. I want them to know the Leo I do, the one with the big heart."

He shakes his head. "It's too late for that. No one here will ever accept me."

"So not true! My family and I already do. Finn and his mother as well. And by the way, Linda wants her job back."

A humorless laugh parts his lips. "I had planned to offer the position to you tonight."

"Me?"

"Don't act so shocked. You wanted it from the minute I told you about it."

He's got me there. I start to respond and he brandishes a hand through the air. "I know you have a secure job with your family business and the bookstore. I only hoped..."

Silence falls as we stare across the long table at each other. "Hoped for what?"

He rises and goes to his desk, returning with a wrapped package. "I want you to have this."

When I touch the paper, the book underneath speaks to me. My fingers shake as realization dawns. "Oh, Leo."

"Open it," he encourages.

I undo the bow. As the first book is revealed, I'm nearly giddy. *Harriet and the Charmed Christmas*. I left it the other day due to all the commotion. The second makes me tear up. "This is for me?"

Harriet and the Magic Monster says "hello."

The copies I've been searching for, here in my hands.

He kneels beside the chair. "I only want to make you happy, Belle. I don't want to stay in this town any longer, and yet, if there was one single thing that could keep me here, it's you."

The fancy dinner forgotten, I drop the books into my lap and sob as I throw my arms around his neck. "Stay then. Stay for me."

He hugs me back, and I hear the books cheer. I feel the presence of love weaving itself around us.

The teapot giggles and the candelabras burn brighter. Jayne wiggles her way in between our bodies and Leo chuckles. As I draw back to look in his face, I see that all of the anger and rage that used to be inside him is gone. In its place is love.

The house breathes a sigh of relief. Magick—beautiful white magick—is in the air.

"I love you, Belle."

I stroke his face and smooth back a random lock of hair. Looking into his green eyes, I know I have found the one thing in life my mother wanted for me.

Love—the greatest magick of all.

I SURE HOPE you enjoyed this story and I'd love to hear from you!

Sign up for my Cozy Clues Mystery Newsletter and be the FIRST to learn about new releases, sales, behind-the-scenes trivia about the book characters, pictures of my pets, and links to insightful and often hilarious *From the Cauldron With Godfrey blog*

Receive a free copy of the Whitethorne Sisters Book of Spells, Recipes, and Crafting Fun when you sign up for my Cozy Clues Mystery Newsletter!

Ready for more magical adventures with the Sherwood Sisters? **Snow is coming in October! Be sure to sign up for the newsletter to get the preorder links as soon as they're available!**

READY FOR MORE MAGICK?

Don't miss the next exciting adventure! Sign up for Nyx's Cozy Clues Mystery Newsletter.

And check out these magical stories!

Sister Witches Of Raven Falls Mystery Series

Sister Witches of Raven Falls Special Collection

Of Potions and Portents
Of Curses and Charms
Of Stars and Spells
Of Spirits and Superstition

Confessions of a Closet Medium Cozy Mystery Series

Confessions of a Closet Medium Special Collection

Pumpkins & Poltergeists
Magic & Mistletoe
Hearts & Haunts
Vows & Vengeance
Cupcakes & Corpses
Tea Leaves & Troubled Spirits

Sister Witches of Story Cove (Formerly Once Upon a Witch) Cozy Mystery Series Coming Fall 2022

Cinder
Belle
Snow
Ruby
Zelle

About the Author

USA Today Bestselling Author Nyx Halliwell who grew up on TV shows like *Buffy the Vampire Slayer* and *Charmed*.

She loves writing stories as much as she loves baking and crafting. She believes in magick and that we each carry it inside us.

She enjoys binge-watching mystery shows with her hubby and reading all types of stories involving magic and animals.

Connect with Nyx today and see pictures of her pets, be the first to know about new books and sales, and find out when Godfrey, the talking cat, has a new blog post! Receive a FREE copy of the Whitethorne Book of Spells and Recipes by signing up for her news-letter http://eepurl.com/gwKHB9

CONNECT WITH NYX TODAY!

Website: nyxhalliwell.com

Email: nyxhalliwellauthor@gmail.com
Bookbub https://www.bookbub.com/profile/nyx-halliwell
Amazon amazon.com/author/nyxhalliwell
Facebook: https://www.facebook.com/NyxHalliwellAuthor/

Sign up for Nyx's Cozy Clues Mystery Newsletter and be the FIRST to learn about new releases, sales, behind-the-scenes trivia about the book characters, pictures of Nyx's pets, and links to insightful and often hilarious *From the Cauldron With Godfrey blog*!

DEAR MAGICAL READER

I hope you enjoyed this story! If you did, and would be so kind, would you leave a review on Goodreads, Bookbub, or your favorite book retailer? I would REALLY appreciate it!

A review lets hundreds, if not thousands, of potential readers know what you enjoyed about the book, and helps them make wise buying choices. It's the best word-of-mouth around.

The review doesn't have to be anything long! Pretend you're sharing the story with a good friend. Pick out one or more characters, scenes, or dialogue that made you smile, laugh, or warmed your heart, and tell them about it. Just a few sentences is perfect!

Blessed be,

Nyx 🤍

9 781948 686693